Penguin Books
Web

John Wyndham was born in 1903. Until 1911 he lived in
Edgbaston, Birmingham, and then in many parts of England.
After a wide experience of the English preparatory school, he
was at Bedales from 1918 till 1921. Careers which he tried
included farming, law, commercial art, and advertising, and
he first started writing short stories intended for sale in
1925. From 1930 till 1939 he wrote stories of various kinds
under different names, almost exclusively for American
publications. He also wrote detective novels. During the war
he was in the Civil Service and afterwards in the Army. In
1946 he went back to writing stories for publication in the
U.S.A. and decided to try a modified form of what is
unhappily known as 'science fiction'. He wrote *The Day of
the Triffids* and *The Kraken Wakes* (both of which have been
translated into several languages), *The Chrysalids, The
Midwich Cuckoos* (filmed as *The Village of the Damned*),
*The Seeds of Time, Trouble with Lichen, The Outward
Urge* (with Lucas Parkes) and *Chocky*, all of which have been
published as Penguins. John Wyndham died in March 1969.

John Wyndham

# WEB

Penguin Books

Penguin Books Ltd, Harmondsworth,
Middlesex, England
Penguin Books, 625 Madison Avenue, New York,
New York 10022, U.S.A.
Penguin Books Australia Ltd, Ringwood,
Victoria, Australia
Penguin Books Canada Ltd, 2801 John Street,
Markham, Ontario, Canada L3R 1B4
Penguin Books (N.Z.) Ltd, 182–190 Wairau Road,
Auckland 10, New Zealand

First published by Michael Joseph 1979
Published in Penguin Books 1980

Typeset, printed and bound in Great Britain by
Hazell Watson & Viney Ltd, Aylesbury, Bucks
Set in Linotype Plantin

# One

The question I find most difficult to answer; the one which always crops up sooner or later when the subject is mentioned, is, approximately:

'But how on earth did *you* come to get yourself mixed up in a crazy affair like this, anyway?'

I don't resent it – partly, I suppose, because it does carry the implication that I can normally be regarded as a reasonably sane citizen – but I do find it scarcely possible to give a reasonably sane answer.

The nearest I can come to an explanation is that I must have been a little off-balance at the time. This could, I imagine, have been the effect of delayed shock: unnoticeable as an aberration, unsuspected by myself yet a shock deep-seated enough to upset my critical sense, to blunt my perceptions and judgement.

I *think* that may have been the cause.

Almost a year before I met Tirrie and so became 'mixed up in the affair' I had a nasty accident.

We were driving – at least, my daughter Mary was actually driving, I was beside her and my wife in the back – along the A272, not far from Etchingham. We were doing, I suppose, about thirty-five when a lorry that must have been travelling at over fifty overtook us. I had a glimpse of it skidding as its back wheels were level with us, another of its enormous load tilting over us . . .

I came round hazily in bed, a week later. They let two more weeks go by before they told me that my wife and Mary were both dead.

I was in that hospital for two months. I came out of it healed as it seemed to me – but dazed and rudderless, with a feeling of unreality, and an entire lack of purpose. I resigned my post. That, I realize now, was the very thing I ought not to have done

– the work would have helped to get me back on balance more than anything else, but at the time it seemed futile, and to require more effort than I could make. So I gave up, convalesced at my sister's home near Tonbridge, and continued to drift along there in a purposeless way, with little to occupy my mind.

I am not used to lack of purpose. I suspect that it creates a vacuum which sooner or later has to be filled – and filled with whatever is available when the negative pressure reaches a crucial point.

That is the only way I can account for the undiscriminating enthusiasm which submerged my commonsense, the surge of un-critical idealism which discounted practical difficulties and seemed to reveal to me, finally and undeniably, my life work and my justification, when I first heard of Lord Foxfield's project.

Alas for disillusion. I would like to convey if I could the whole bright prospect as I saw it then. It was such stuff as dreams are made of. But now it is gone, sicklied o'er with the pale cast of cynicism. I look at myself as at someone else moving half-awake ... and yet ... and yet at times I feel that there was the spark of an idea, an ideal behind it that could have started a flame – had the Fates shown us one touch of benevolence.

The original idea, or the core of the idea, that grew into the Foxfield Project seems to have occurred spontaneously and sim-ultaneously in the minds of his Lordship and Walter Tirrie. The former publicly claims its authorship; the latter was known to claim privately that it was inspired by him. It seems possible that it was a spark thrown off in the course of conversation between them which ignited in both, and was industriously fanned by both minds.

Walter was, by profession, an architect, but perhaps more widely known as an ardent correspondent and persistent setter-right of the world in the columns of several weekly reviews. From this he had graduated to being a moderately familiar figure speaking on platforms devoted to numerous causes. There may even have been some truth in his claim to have introduced the idea to Lord Foxfield, for if one takes the trouble to track back over his letters in the correspondence columns over a few years it is possible to find not only faint inklings of the plan, but also of his feeling that he was the man, *Dei gratia*, to realize it. Though it would seem that it was only after his meeting with his Lordship that the insubstantial fragments of the idea began to fall into form.

This possibly took place because his Lordship could contribute more than mere form; he could give it expression, endow it with money, put his weight behind it, and pull strings where necessary.

And why was he willing to back it in all these ways?

Well, one can dismiss straight away all the subtle schemes and dubious intentions with which gossip credited him. His motive was quite uncomplicated and ingenuous : he was, quite simply, a man in search of a memorial.

It is a desire that is not even unusual among rich, elderly men. Indeed, to quite a number of them there appears to come a revelatory day when they look at all those comma-spaced triplets of figures, and are suddenly pierced by awareness of their inability to take it with them, whereupon they are seized by the desire to convert those hollow noughts into a tangible, and usually autographed, token of their successes.

This mood has come upon them through the ages, but of late it has become less easy to fulfil – or perhaps one should say to fulfil it with the desirable distinction of benefaction – than it was even in the days of the old tycoons. The State, now so pervasive, tends to abrogate to itself even the function of benefactor. Education is no longer an outlet; it is free, at all levels, for all. The erstwhile poor – now the lower-income brackets – are housed at municipal expense. Playing-fields are provided by the ratepayers. Public, even peripatetic, libraries are subsidized by county councils. The working-man – now the worker – prefers overtime and the telly to Clubs and Institutes.

A man may, it is true, still found a College or two in some University, but this does not entirely suit every donor's benefactory urge – for one thing, if there is felt to be a need for such a College someone will finance one anyway; for another, in these days of Government interference no intention or stipulation would be safe. Ministerial decision could easily modify one's intended seat of higher learning into just another spring-board of knowhow, overnight. In fact the field for worthy acts of eleemosynary commemoration has been so sadly reduced that Lord Foxfield spent some two years after the urge struck him in a vain search for a goodwill project which, if he did not undertake it himself, was unlikely to be adopted by any Ministry, Council, Corporation, Institution or Society.

It was a period of great strain for his secretary. Word appeared to have got round, as word will, that his Lordship was ripening for a good touch, and skilful defences were needed. It took a highly plausible suggestion, or the sanction of a very influential Society, to carry a proponent past the barriers and into the Presence, and remarkably few of the schemes put forward held any interest for his Lordship when he heard them.

'I have been discovering,' he is reported to have said, 'what an astonishing amount of goodwill there is in this age – and that most of it is woolly. People have a noticeably strong sense of duty towards their ancestors – more than ninety per cent of the propositions I receive are interested in conserving for the sake of conservation, which is felt, *ipso facto*, to be a good thing, and their sense of duty towards their posterity seems to consist solely in preserving the past.

'Also, they appear to be unbalanced about animals. I should not be in the least surprised if someone were to put up to me to-morrow a thoroughly humane and well-concerned proposal for the rehabilitation on a national scale of old roadside drinking-troughs for horses.'

It would appear, however, that one serious hindrance in his Lordship's search for an outlet was his own vanity. For Lord Foxfield was an individualist. He had made his own way by exploiting his own abilities according to his own judgement, and done it with a success which rendered it contrary to his nature to submerge himself in, or even to be closely identified with, a conventional Society for good works. Indeed, he had been known to point out from time to time that had certain social achievements been introduced anonymously, or even by corporate sponsors, they would have lacked the character, as well as the weight of example, which names such as Carnegie, Peabody, Ford, Nuffield, Nobel, Gulbenkian among others had given them. And, indeed it was clearly the challenge raised by such exemplars that caused him to seek a medium that would express – and, incidentally be seen to express – his desire to benefit mankind by tidying up some neglected corner of its feckless world.

How he came to make the acquaintance of Walter Tirrie is not recorded. Possibly he sought him out. Walter was almost constantly in a state of inky vendetta with other correspondents upon one or other of our social inadequacies, and it seems not unlikely that some of these exchanges, catching his Lordship's eye and fancy, may have led to a meeting. At any rate, it is fairly certain that Walter was not among those who queued up with a prepared scheme needing only financial aid. Rather it appears, as I have said, that their purpose simply grew, inkling out of their conversation, enfilading their minds, and establishing itself as the Project.

And, once this stage was reached, all other propositions or organizations lost, from that moment, any chance they may have had of tapping the Foxfield wealth. His Lordship became finally uninterested in proposals to pour money down other people's drains; he had invented, or discovered, a culvert quite his own.

The intention, though ambitious, was in essence simple – in fact, in essence it was unoriginal. Its difference lay in the intention and the ability to remove it from the ineffective minds of dreamers, and give it practical existence.

It was to set up a free, politically independent community endowed with the opportunity, and the means, to create a new climate of living.

'The ideal start would consist of a clean slate inscribed with just two words – Knowledge and Reason,' Lord F is said to have proclaimed. 'Unfortunately that is a long way from being practicable. The best that can be done is to provide a place where there is freedom to question the axioms, the prejudices, traditions, loyalties, and all those attitudes implanted in us before we could think, which together make us citizens of the world as it is, instead of becoming citizens of the world as it might be. The purpose will be to break the chain we drag behind us linking us perpetually through the generations right back to primitive man and beyond: to throw off the burden of inherited archaic lore.

'Most of the conflict in the world reflects the conflict in our minds as we strive to move forward while the brakes of false doctrines, superstitions, obsolete standards, and misconceived ambitions are always at work on us. These checks are built-in, we cannot free ourselves from them, but we can loosen them for others.

If we provide the right conditions, as free from contamination as possible, there is hope that in a generation, or in two or more generations, they may cease to bind.'

He went on to envisage the community growing and developing, gaining recognition by gifted men of all races as a haven where one could think and work, untroubled by financial, national or other vested pressures. A new culture would arise there, a culture lit by the knowledge of its own day, with no shadowy lurking-places for the clutch-fingered brain-washing ghosts of the irrational past. In the fresh air of a new uplands minds would have space for unstinted growth in a climate where they could expand into full flower.

From small beginnings there would grow a city; in due course would follow The Enlightened State. Men and women who perceived that the world could not muddle along in the old way for much longer, and that the break with the old thinking must be made before it was too late, would turn towards the new State with hope. To it, with its opportunity to think and work, would flock the future Einsteins, Newtons, Curies, Flemings, Rutherfords, Oppenheimers. One day, perhaps, it could become the mind-powerhouse of the world . . .

And, naturally, carved into its foundations would be the name of Frederick, First Baron Foxfield . . .

In the early stages, however, the name of Lord Foxfield was, for various reasons, not associated with the Project. He preferred to use Walter Tirrie as his front-man. Consequently, it was through Walter that I first became acquainted with the scheme.

The introduction was contrived by some friends of mine, out of kindly concern, I believe. They knew that I was unoccupied and without interests, and, possibly prompted by my sister who was also worried by my state, invited me to dinner to meet him.

Walter was at that time already well involved in the preparations. Not the least of his troubles was the recruitment of suitable personnel or, indeed, any personnel. Letters to his usual correspondence columns giving the outline of the plan, with an invitation to any interested persons to write to him for further details had produced disappointing results. Looking back now I am not greatly surprised. It must have seemed an unrealistic proposition, and I have no doubt that had I come across it in the ordinary way I should have dismissed it as a crackpot venture.

Listening to him talking of it with confidence – and the untroubled assurance of adequate backing – gave a different impression. I was, as I have explained, in a susceptible state, and very soon I found myself kindling to his enthusiasm.

During the night that followed the kindling process continued. In fact somewhere in the small hours I was seeing visions of the Enlightened State in being. Unfortunately I cannot recall any of the details now. All that lingers is an impression of a place lit by a golden glow, suffused by a spirit of goodwill, hope and comradeship. (I know it sounds like a show of Russian posters depicting the future of the New Lands, but for all I know the Russians may feel as I felt then.) I was aware of a sense of revelation – as if I had been stumbling along in a half-lit world, and suddenly had been shown a brightly lighted way stretching out before me. I was filled, too, with a sense of incredulity at my own blindness hitherto – at everyone's blindness. The path was so plain, so obvious. Get away, right away, from all the clinging briars of usage, convention, habit – and, in a clean new place help to build the foundations of a clean new world. Could there be anything better to do with one's life than that . . .?

The next day I rang up Walter, and arranged to meet him again. From that moment I was in it.

Soon I was in it to a privileged extent. I knew that Lord Foxfield was behind it, and Walter took me to see him.

He was not an impressive man – no, that is putting it too badly. He had a side calculated to impress: assured, slightly pompous, a little short-tempered, but that was his public, professional aspect; he donned it like a business-suit. Off-duty, so to speak, he was not afraid of showing, or possibly unconscious of showing, an odd naïvety. I could never get used to the changes from one to the other.

It was the executive manner he was wearing when he greeted me. The look he gave me had the appearance of being keen and appraising – whether it really was, or not, I still do not know. But presently, when we got on to the subject of the Project he dropped the businesslike front, and let his genuine enthusiasm take over.

'Walter, here, will have given you the outline of our plan, Mr

Delgrange,' he said, 'so you'll know that the idea is to begin with a pioneer party, to be joined by more recruits later on. It is to my mind extremely important that the original group should start along the right lines, and form the right habits of mind. If the wrong observances, wrong attitudes and outlook are able to establish themselves at the beginning, the task of eradicating them to create the kind of society we have in mind will add greatly to our difficulties.

'Now, I have taken the trouble to find out about you, Mr Delgrange. I know in general the views you are credited with. I know that you have some standing as a social historian, and I have read with interest two of your books. They have shown me that you are an intelligent observer of social trends, and I have come to the conclusion, and I know Walter agrees with me, that your trained observation could be of immense assistance to us, in the early stages at least, in determining the best forms for our institutions, as well as in steering the community towards those forms – and away from less desirable forms which may tend to arise.'

He continued to embroider this theme at some length, and I ended the evening with the rather dazed realization that I had been given the task of drawing up and submitting for his approval a provisional draft constitution for the Enlightened State – as well as the job of applying it in practice later on.

It kept me busy for some months.

This is no place to go into the details of the organization of the pioneer party. Nor do I know a lot, for it was not my job. I was vaguely aware that Walter was disappointed by the responses to his call for recruits, and felt that he was expecting too much. He seemed surprised to discover the scarcity of intellectuals who were also good practical men. And then, when he had relinquished the thought of finding them combined in the same individual, surprised again that neither type was presenting itself with the readiness he had hoped for.

I did my best to arouse interest in some of my friends, but found invariably that it stopped well short of my desire to take part in the venture. I was much too taken up with the Project at that time to perceive that their chief reaction to my enthusiasm was concern on my behalf, even when they tried, as some of them did, to dissuade me. Anyway, recruitment was Walter's department, and he was not very expansive about its progress.

It was not long after my introduction to Lord Foxfield that Walter disappeared for a couple of months in search of a suitable site for the Project. I heard nothing from him during this time, nor was he very communicative when he returned. This, he gave me to understand, was for reasons of policy. He would say nothing of the location except that he was satisfied that it was ideal for the purpose. Negotiations for acquiring it were, he explained, going to be delicate; it would be best if as few people as possible were aware of them until they were complete. With that I had to be satisfied.

Still, it was clear that things were moving. He now had an office with a number of staff who always appeared to be furiously busy whenever I called there, and he himself had taken on the manner of the confident executive.

During the nine months that followed Walter's return I had a number of meetings with Lord Foxfield. I found him easier to get on with than I had anticipated – I had suspected that he would have ideas of his own to put forward, and possibly insist upon. It was pleasant to discover that his views on a workable form of democracy accorded well with my own. The points he took me up on were, for the most part, perceptive, and led to few disagreements, none of them on major considerations, so that I gradually came to realize that his interest lay in being kept informed, rather than in steering. His desire, in fact, was to see his Project started on what appeared to be the right lines. His continual response when we did disagree on details was: 'All right. Try it. But keep it *flexible*. You must keep it *flexible*. It is a changing world. We don't want to encumber ourselves with something as rigid as the American Constitution. We want a humanist constitution, one that will work without a legislature.' And in my enthusiasm, I agreed with him: it all seemed so simple, so rational.

Then came an evening when he told me.

'It's gone through. We've got our site. Signed and sealed today.'

We raised our glasses and drank to a long, successful life for the Project.

'And now, at last, may I know where it is?' I asked.

'It is a place, an island, called Tanakuatua,' he told me.

It was the first time I heard the name. (And he pronounced it Tanner-kooer-tooer instead of Tanna-kwah-twah, as we came to know it.)

'Oh,' I said, rather blankly. 'Where is it?'

'Lies south-east of the Midsummers,' he explained.

Which left me as unknowledgeable as before – except that it suggested somewhere in the other hemisphere.


Thereafter, with a known destination before us, the scheme took on a new reality. The pace of preparations increased. I found myself pressed into assisting Walter, and even sat in on some of his interviews with prospective candidates.

I cannot say I was impressed with the quality of the material that was coming forward to offer itself, but took some consolation that this would be only the pioneer group. Once the Project was established, once there existed a going concern, something one could come to and join, the appeal would be much stronger.

Undoubtedly Walter, and the rest of us, had underestimated the difficulty of assembling any kind of nucleus for such a venture. After all, the fit fit; it is the misfit who is free. The man whose gifts have won him a place in our system, but is prepared to throw it away in order to take a chance on an idealistic whim is understandably rare. So most of the applicants were only too palpably misfits of one kind or another. Not pioneer material – not community material, either. It must have been discouraging for Walter who conducted most of the interviews, but by now he was too deeply immersed in other aspects of the operation to let it weigh on him. He had aimed at a personnel of fifty, but was prepared to content himself with forty-six.

In the meantime, with the purchase of Tanakuatua safely concluded, Lord Foxfield had emerged into the open as the backer of the Project.

Acknowledgement of his sponsorship of the Project had been more or less forced upon him in order to forestall a more unpleasant kind of publicity.

There is an Opposition technique which, though trite, is still tediously employed. One selects an event which is deemed to have a suitable appeal for public indignation, and a slant which harmonizes with the Party's views. At a dull moment one draws the attention of a national newspaper to it. If it looks promising, and nothing more interesting intervenes, the newspaper adopts it as a Cause, and launches it with a splash. The Party then agrees to one's putting down a Question, indicating the newspaper articles as evidence of the people's passionate concern over the Government's latest iniquity. Thus the newspaper is shown to be the public's trusty watchdog, one's Party as its ready champion, and, if all goes well, the Government ought, once again, to be embarrassed.

In the case of the Tanakuatua sale, which was chosen as suitable material for the employment of this technique, there was a hitch. It had been decided that the angle: 'Outrageous scandal of secret barter of British territory to private interests' ought to make quite useful trouble-fodder, and the *Daily Tidings* was not unwilling to oblige. Indeed, its editor was considering how it could most effectively be handled, when he received information drawing his attention to several relevant facts: (a) that Tirrie, the purchaser of Tanakuatua, was a front-man for Lord Foxfield, (b) that there was a long standing friendship between Lord F and his Lordship, the proprietor of the *Tidings*, (c) that his latter Lordship had, in circumstances that were not dissimilar, himself acquired an island in the Caribbean.

Understandably the *Tidings*' interest in the matter then waned. Furthermore, it was allowed to be known that his (Press) Lordship would regard any playing up of the subject by any other newspaper as an unfriendly act. As a consequence, the Opposition turned to fresh woes and scandals new, and Tanakuatua's change of ownership received no more notice than an occasional factual paragraph here and there.

Lord Foxfield's interest, however, was now known, and since that fact could no longer affect the price he had paid for the island, he was not unwilling to identify himself as the begetter of the venture.

The press, however, had its revenge, as it always does. The venture got a silly-season write-up. The coverage was slanted to give the impression of an old man's senile whim, to present the members of the expedition as a bunch of irresponsibles for whom

15

life in a properly ordered society was not good enough – and by implication to make the stay-at-home readers themselves feel sensible and normal. We all had a trying time for a while, and five of the volunteers resigned, bringing our total force down to forty, but when we were no longer a novelty the newspapers' interest in us waned, to revive only briefly at the time of our departure.

On the eve of that departure we assembled at a hotel in Bloomsbury. Most of us had never met before. There was a noticeable tendency among the members to eye one another with caution, even with misgiving. I must admit that even my enthusiasm felt the strain. Walter and I did our best with introductions to induce something of a party spirit, but it was heavy going. We looked, I imagine, more like a flock of bewildered sheep than a brave band of pioneers-oh. But, we told ourselves, jollity would have been equally out of place. After all, we were embarking on a serious mission . . .

I myself seem in my recollection to have been in a state of dichotomy. I can recall moments of depression alternating with phases of positive exaltation. In fact I can recall a wondering look in the eyes of some of those I spoke to, as if they found my enthusiasm a little alarming.

Drinks and a good dinner did something to ease and unloosen us, and there were even signs of a sense of team spirit beginning to show, when at the end of it Lord Foxfield rose to give us his valedictory address.

I think I will quote from that. It will give, perhaps, a better impression of his vision for the future than I have conveyed.

'God,' began Lord Foxfield, rather surprisingly, for him. 'God, we have been assured, created man in His own image. His own image – let us consider what that means.' He did so, at some length, coming to the conclusion that the image meant the true image. He continued :

'Now, it is not for man to select which of the powers latent in that image he will employ, nor which he will reject. To do so would be tantamount to declaring that God had included certain powers by mistake – or that man knew better than God which powers he should employ, a supposition that puts us on a slippery slope indeed. For surely if God had not intended a power to be used, He could have included it only by accident, or for a mischievous purpose – a proposition which, I imagine, few would accept.

'Thus we must accept that by including certain powers in man's make-up God implicitly laid upon him the duty not of approving or disapproving of these gifts, but the duty of employing them all, to the best of his ability.

'It follows, therefore, since man's image is God's, God must have intended man to become like God.

'Why else should He give him His own image? He has, after all used countless other images for His less capable creations: consequently, by choosing to use His own image He must – unless He deliberately made a spurious image of Himself – have laid upon man the obligation to become as godlike in manner as in form.

'Now, this is not a novel deduction. Many rulers, from the earliest times up to the present day, have perceived it – and have, in consequence become aware of, and proclaimed, their personal deification and divine rights. Being, however, strong individualists they have interpreted this divinity as setting themselves apart from, and above, other men. Unfortunately, also, they have tended to model their conduct upon that of the captious God of the Old Testament – with unhappy results for others of their kind.

'They were not wrong. Their mistake, or blind-spot, if you prefer it, was their failure in logical perception, their inability to see that since mankind was created in the image of God, the destiny and duty of being godlike cannot be restricted to concern simply a few selected persons: it must fall equally upon *all* who are in the image, which is to say, upon all mankind.

'We have long been aware that man is the mightiest species in the creation. During the recent centuries, and particularly in our time, we have seen spectacular increases in his power. Even now his domination of much of his environment is godlike: and his potentialities are unguessable.

'Indeed, he may have exceeded divine expectations in some directions already, for, though the ability of God to annihilate Himself is theologically debatable, man has undebatably achieved the ability to destroy *himself*, and his world as well.

'This capacity alone should serve to make it clear that the time has now come for us to cease to behave like a lot of irresponsible children letting off fireworks in a crowded hall. It was always stupid; now it has become too dangerous.

'We have now acquired the knowledge and the means to construct for ourselves a rational and mentally healthy form of society. We can adapt much of our environment to our needs – and even, if necessary, much of ourselves to our environment. We have become able, if we wish and so order it, to live not by destruction of, not in conflict with, not as parasites upon the world about us, but in harmony with it, creating a symbiosis with the forces of nature: guiding and directing, but also bestowing as we receive. We have reached a stage where we can – and must, if we are to survive – stop living with the fecklessness of animals, and take charge of our own destiny. If we are afraid to become men like gods – then we shall perish . . .

'That is what this expedition is about. It is not – as the popular press would have people think – a flight from reality. It is not seeking a lotus-land, an Eden, or even a utopia. It is the small seed of a great intention.

'You are setting out to plant that seed in a brave new world. To care for it and coax it until it produces fair, fresh, uncontaminated crops to sustain a new society liberated from superstition, purged of blind faiths and ignorant beliefs, freed at last from the cruelty, misery, and frustration that these things have plagued mankind with from time immemorial . . .'

There was quite a lot more of it with quite a variety of simile and metaphor – as well as a little confusion, some might have felt, in his angles of approach to his subject. Nevertheless, the gist was clear: 'The knowledge and the means to create a sane society exist. Here is your opportunity to use them. Now go to it, and good luck to you.'

And, indeed, Lord F might well have contented himself with some such succinctness, for there were some in his audience who did not find it easy to combine his advocacy of rationalism with the unlooked-for prospect of their apotheosis.

However, it was his Lordship's day. He had paid a very pretty penny to bring it about, and it would cost him a lot more yet, so he was heard out with patience and occasional applause right to

his final exhortation to us to bear in mind the words of Henley:
'I am the Master of my fate: I am the Captain of my soul'.

There exists a coloured photograph of our party assembled the
next day on the deck of the *Susannah Dingley*, taken shortly
before she sailed. We number thirty-eight, having been reduced
to that number by a couple of not entirely convincing indisposi-
tions developed overnight.

We are not a gathering that the unprompted observer would
instantaneously have recognized as the Founding Fathers (and
Mothers) of a new era. Yet what would be? So many people
manage to look unimpressive until they have made their impression.

And, after all, given a fair chance, we might have made it –
some of us ...

The dominant figure in the photograph is undoubtedly Mrs
Brinkley. This is due in part to the prominence of the bulging
travel-bag which she clutches, a massive affair decorated with
what appears to be a Japanese hunting tartan, but even without
it her own broad, beaming, brood-flanked presence would take
the eye. One feels that, whatever the ideals and hopes of the rest
of us may be, Deborah Brinkley knows just what she wants; it
is more babies, and she is ready to go on cheerfully accumulating
them on Tanakuatua, or wherever else the tides of life may carry
her. This, and the presence of her husband beside her, looking
the sturdy, capable farmer he is, has the effect of making her the
most confidence-inspiring figure in the picture.

Alicia Hardy, who can be seen close by, talking earnestly to
one of the Brinkley children, gives us a touch of distinction.

But there can be no doubt that it is Marilyn Slaight (Mrs
Slaight) who *thinks* she is stealing the picture. In a spectacularly
inappropriate going-away outfit, a pose picked up from a fashion
magazine, and with a great big smile for all the world, she is
clearly self-cast as the belle of the voyage. She stands next to
Horace Tupple, his chubby, babyish face already topping a vivid
beach-shirt. A more clearly marked life and soul of any party it
would be hard to find. I wonder to this day how those two managed to get under Walter's guard. Horace himself apparently got

to wondering the same thing during the following week or two, for he decided to skip the ship at Panama and make his way home. It is remarkable how wise a fool can be.

The small man in the front row frowning at the camera from under his cap is Joe Shuttleshaw. He was a useful carpenter, but, at a glance, a born chip-bearer; beside him is his wife, Diane, as obviously a born husband-bearer. Beyond her Jennifer Felling, the nurse, has rather the effect of a Derain included in a bunch of Matisses. The other Jennifer, Jennifer Deeds, is looking serenely dedicated.

Walter Tirrie is there, of course. He is holding himself a little apart from the rest of us. Something, perhaps the work of preparation, perhaps the angle of the light, has given his face a chiselled look that I had not been aware of before. Also, he has taken on in an undefinable way an air of leadership, and regards the camera with an air of challenge.

Away on the right, Jamie McIngoe the engineer, wears a slight smile – though whether it is caused by Walter, or by the occasion, or by his own thoughts is hard to tell.

Next to him stands Camilla Cogent. She seems withdrawn into her own reflections, unaware of camera or occasion alike: there, but not with us.

I, Arnold Delgrange, am away on the other side, seen in profile. With my gaze distant, and my expression rapt, I look a little 'sent'. And at that moment I confess I was. Even now I can catch glimpses of the mood that filled me then. The rest of the party's feet are planted on the steel deck-plates of the *Susannah Dingley* – but mine are treading the planks of a new *Argo*. The sullied waters of the Thames eddy viscously beneath the others, but I am gazing far beyond them, to a new Aegean, gold and caerulean in the sun. I am setting out to turn a vision into a reality, to see the world's great age begin anew, to play my part in contriving that:

> Another Athens shall arise,
> And to remoter time
> Bequeath, like sunset to the skies,
> The splendour of its prime.

In that moment I am seeing even more – a new, distant archipelago in which a whole lost world shall flare, phoenix-like, into re-birth . . .

Alas for the sweet songs the sirens sang!

There we stand. Tom Conning, Jeremy Brandon, David Kamp, and the rest. All kinds of us, from Arnold Delgrange, the dreamer, to Charles Brinkley, the farmer — and any man's choice for the title of colonist-most-likely-to-succeed.

It is a saddening photograph. We may not look much, certainly we do not present the appearance of a galaxy of talents, but all of us then were filled with high hopes. And the idea that had brought us together was much greater than ourselves.

Ah, well — it will be tried again, I suppose. Men have been setting out these thousand years and more in search of freedom ... Yes, they will try again — and next time I hope the Fates will be with them, not against them ...

# Two

So we sailed for Tanakuatua.

And this seems an appropriate place to give some account of our destination.

When the *Susannah Dingley* raised her anchor and set out, all that I or indeed any of us, except Walter who had found the place for us, knew of Tanakuatua was that it was a small, uninhabited island too insignificant to be recorded at all in most general atlases, but discoverable in some of the larger and more conscientious ones as an out-of-scale dot in the large blue spread of the Pacific Ocean, located in the region of 9° N, 170° W.

There were some pictures of it, too, taken at intervals over the last seventy years. These for practical purposes, however, can be considered as one picture since each photographer has been struck by the same scenic quality of precisely the same view. It gives a vista looking north-east as seen from a ship moored in the lagoon. There is a line of curving white beach hedged by undergrowth from which springs a pallisade of palms, thickly backed by more palms and trees of other kinds. It is only the background that distinguishes this aspect from that of a thousand other beaches: the twin hills united by a high saddle that identify it as Tanakuatua.

These hills do not immediately suggest volcanic activity, but both contain craters. The northern one (that on the left in the pictures) is Rara, long choked and overgrown; the other, Monu, hold a pool of boiling mud, and from halfway down its southern side gushes a hot spring of clear water. It is probably a very long time since either of the craters was other than it is now. There are no legends of any activity there.

Indeed, there seem to be few legends of any kind about the island. It is as if it existed in its isolation without a history until less than two centuries ago. Even since then the record is fragmentary, but I have, since my return, been at considerable pains to find out what I can about it from a variety of sources and feel that this is the best place to include the result of my researches. They do at least go some way towards explaining a factor which puzzled some of us from the start of the voyage: that is the availability of an uninhabited, but richly fertile island.

In those atlases which do notice it, Tanakuatua is usually shown as included in the Midsummer Islands group. This was always misleading, and later became inaccurate. In the first place, it lies five hundred miles from the nearest of them, and about one hundred and fifty miles from its nearest, and smaller, neighbour, Oahomu. One suspects that both these islands may well have been brought into the Midsummers' zone for the sake of tidiness by those who draw those sweeping, territorial dotted lines on maps of the Pacific Ocean, since they are still more remote from any other island group. It is, moreover, not inconceivably the existence of these lines which caused them at one time to become a responsibility of the Midsummers' administration. Stranger things than that have happened in Colonial history.

In the days of early exploration both islands appear to have been elusive. Unlike most islands in the region they were unnoticed even by Captain Cook, for though, on his second voyage, in 1774, he visited (and named appropriately to the season of his visit) the Midsummers, neither the log of the *Resolution*, nor that of the *Adventure*, makes mention of any such outlying islands, though one would have thought one or other of them to lie close enough to his course to be observed.

It is not, however, until twenty years later that the discovery of an island that can scarcely have been other than Tanakuatua is recorded.

In 1794 Captain Sleason, of the *Purpose*, noted in his journal: '7th day of April at six of the clock in the morning, the wind backing and falling to calm, brought upon us a thick fog. In this we continued drifting three days. On the morning of the 10th April came on a strong wind from the West which drove off the fog, but, freshening to a gale, forced us in heavy weather far to eastward of our course. This, likewise, held for three days. In the night of the 13th–14th the gale abated, the morning breaking serene, with the sea fallen again near to calm, and the wind Westerly yet, but now very light.

'By first light we sighted land at some three leagues distant, bearing E.S.E. Making closer we discovered it to be an Island of no great size, rising in the centre to a mountain of low height having the form of two humps joined by a ridge. The vegetation is abundant, palms and other trees, together with bushes thickly covering all but the upper parts of the Mountain.

'At our approach, sea birds in great numbers flew out to attend us, and a school of dolphins rode to our bows, but we could perceive no sign of human habitation.

'The Western side of this Island is set about with a stout reef having a number of islets in it, and also several navigable passages. One of these we sounded and successfully essayed. Having anchored in the lagoon, I sent the cutter ashore, with water kegs.

'The boat crew found the Island not to be uninhabited, as it had appeared, for, having discovered a stream and followed it up a short way for clear water, they came upon a small clearing. Set about this were seven or eight huts, exceedingly mean and poorly constructed, being in the main of pieces of bark lashed together. The condition of this place was so filthy as to set up a noisome stench. At the centre of the clearing was a pit of ashes, with several large stones of the kind which natives of these parts use for their cooking, lying therein. One of our men, thinking the place long deserted, found this not to be so, and suffered a slightly scorched foot.

'The boatswain, then coming up, was of the opinion that it had not been deserted above an hour or two, though we had seen no smoke.

'Some of the huts contained wooden tools of poor workmanship, also some rudely contrived nets which were judged to be for fishing. In one hut was found a human leg bone decorated in part by carving, and a stone knife lying among chips of bone from the work. Also in this hut was a human skull, more recently fresh than the leg bone, and declared by the boatswain, though out of what experience I know not, to have been not above a week severed.

'After several journeys, our watering then being sufficient, the crew came aboard, having had no sight of any of the natives.'

The general location of this island and the reference to the double-summitted mountain leave little doubt that it was Tanakuatua. Its rediscovery and the true charting of its position, however, had to wait until it was visited by H.M.S. *Pertinax* in 1820. And in the twenty-six years that had passed since Captain Sleason wrote his account, conditions there seem to have changed.

The *Pertinax* made a preliminary circumnavigation of the island noting that the eastern and northern coasts were rocky and inhospitable, offering neither convenient landing places, nor good anchorage, and that a strong reef starting from the southernmost point enclosed a lagoon which bounded almost all the west coast. The ship did not attempt a passage of the reef, but dropped anchor just outside it, within sight of a beach on which a number of canoes was drawn up.

A party of about fifty natives, armed with spears, gathered on the beach, in lively conference. They then launched six of the canoes and made across the lagoon towards the *Pertinax*. A little short of the passage through the reef, however, they paused, and rested their paddles. The canoes came together. There was another, more sober, conference during which heads turned now and then towards the ship. After this exchange of second thoughts they turned back, making energetically for the shore where, after pulling up the canoes, they withdrew into the trees, and disappeared entirely.

A shore-party, landed from the *Pertinax*, found a village of huts entirely deserted. Among the possessions left behind by the natives they came upon a rusty pistol, several sailors' knives, four brass belt-buckles, and a number of metal buttons, as well as less surprising objects such as a row of skulls on the lintels of the largest hut, and a number of bone ornaments and barbs.

In course of further exploration they noticed a cross erected upon a small headland further along the coast. This they found to be made of pieces of planking, clearly from some ship, nailed together, set upright, and roughly carved with the letters R.I.P. Digging in front of it in the hope of finding something that would identify the grave, they unearthed, instead of the remains they expected, a bottle containing a folded piece of paper. On this was written in a brown pigment, thought to be blood:

While returning, the *Pertinax* party suffered an ambush by the
natives. One man was nastily wounded by a spear, but three of
the attackers fell to the muskets, whereupon the rest fled, leaving two of their number as prisoners.

From these captives the sailors later took the name of the island
to be, as nearly as they could pronounce it (and assuming that it
was indeed a name, and not some kind of invocation or curse)
Tanakuatua. Accordingly it was so entered in the records, and
has since remained.

Documents in the Record Office show that a ship named *Fortitude* did in fact sail from Deptford on the 2nd August 1811
bound for Botany Bay with a cargo of one hundred and forty-
two convicts. She never arrived, and was later assumed to be lost
at sea. In the list of convicts sentenced to transportation aboard
her occur the names:

> James Bare, of London, for the forging
> of a postage frank, value 6 pence.
>
> Edward Timson, of Shepton in Somer-
> set, for combining to maintain the rate
> of wages.
>
> Henry Davies, of Lewes in Sussex, for
> theft of a fowl, value 7 pence.

One of the members of the ship's crew is recorded as Samuel
Hodges, of Rye, in Sussex.

The Ship's last reported port of call was Otaheite (later known
as Tahiti). She sailed from there on the 15th April 1812, whereafter all trace of her was lost.

Tanakuatua was now officially in existence on the Admiralty

charts, but continued to be rarely visited, and then almost exclusively by ships driven off course, and finding themselves in need of water and fresh vegetables. There was, occasionally, some barter, but as the island had a reputation for treacherous inhabitants addicted to cannibalism, such visits were more usually in the nature of raids.

Thus there had been no exploration, and little more was known of the place than could be seen from the sea before 1848, when a survey party went ashore from H.M.S. *Finder*. It reported the natives as being 'painted with patterns, much ornamented with shells and shell-work, and with some small pieces of coarse cloth worn more for decoration than for modesty. Most of the men wear, also, pieces of bone thrust through large slits in their ear-lobes, and often more slender bone needles through the septum of the nose, frequently projecting several inches on either side. Their faces are tattooed in an unsightly fashion in order to give the appearance of great ferocity.'

When this fierce appearance, accompanied by loud shouts, menacing gestures and a brandishing of spears, failed to deter the approach of the survey party with its escort of marines, the natives seemed at first astonished, and then to suffer loss of heart. And as the marines raised their rifles preparatory to firing an intimidating volley over their heads, they immediately ran away, and hid among the trees where they remained until they were coaxed back by offers of presents.

With formal defiance thus disposed of, the party found them shy and suspicious. The only other hostile incident occurred when half-a-dozen of the party found their path barred by a group of some ten natives. All but one were armed with metal-tipped spears. The exception held a rusty musket. He lifted this unreliable weapon, and pointing it in the general direction of the ship's party, raised his voice, apparently commanding it to fire. When it did not, he and his companions looked disconcerted. He tried again, and then, with a gesture of disgust, threw it on the ground, and the whole band scampered off into the bushes. Thereafter the survey went peacefully, though it was strictly forbidden for any man to straggle alone.

Tanakuatua was duly mapped. It is, in general, pear-shaped, with a length of eight miles and a width slightly over five. A small island, Hinuati, stands about a mile and a half off its southern tip, and has an area of some hundred and fifty acres. Along the reef are a dozen or so smaller islets varying in size from half an acre up to one of twelve acres. The soil is of volcanic origin, rich in mineral salts, productive of good taro crops, bread fruit, coconuts, and a variety of vegetables. The latter were unexpectedly found to include potatoes which were assumed to have been salvaged from a wreck, possibly that of *Fortitude*, and planted by castaways.

The adult population of Tanakuatua appeared at this time to be fairly small, possibly little more than one hundred and fifty, though deserted village sites suggested that it had recently been larger. The habits, conditions, and practices of the natives were reported as being mean, crude, and sordid to a repulsive degree. The officer in charge of the survey-party considered them to be the most primitive savages he had ever encountered, but in this he differed from the ship's doctor who maintained that they were an example of degeneration induced by prolonged interbreeding.

The report did not doubt that the island, if intelligently cultivated, was capable of supporting a considerable population as well as producing copra and other trade commodities in useful quantity. Having regard, however, to the necessary amount of preliminary work, the capital required for it, the unsuitability of the natives for such work and the consequent need to import labour, the small size of the crops likely to be produced during several initial years, and, above all, the isolation of Tanakuatua from all usual trade routes, it was very doubtful whether any attempt to exploit the island's potentialities could prove worthwhile.

Having thus summed up Tanakuatua's relevance to the nineteenth-century world, H.M.S. *Finder* then sailed away northwesterly to survey and, in due course, to issue a still less favourable report on the island of Oahomu.

But if Tanakuatua was without importance in the world at large, it did not follow that the converse was true, and although the tempo was slow, the island was to experience more of it in the next sixty years than in some previous thousands.

In or about the year 1852 there was an invasion. Details are sketchy, but it appears to have been conducted by a force some three hundred strong, in a fleet of canoes. Who they were and where they came from – beyond their statement that their ancestral island lay somewhere towards the setting sun – is obscure, but from the fact that they brought with them their wives and families, and even fowls and small livestock houses in huts supported catamaran fashion upon lashed-together canoes, it is clear that they were engaged in purposeful migration.

Hostilities were brief, seemingly about half a day long, whereafter the residents' resistance, demoralized by the invaders' prowess and confidence, collapsed entirely, never to revive.

The newcomers brought a superior technology. In place of the groups of filthy bark hovels they built villages of thatched huts. They cleared spaces for taro patches and planted coconut groves; they laid out gardens with several kinds of vegetables, and made it clear in many other ways that they had come to stay.

The two bloods mingled. Occasional ships putting in for one reason or another contributed new strains, too, so that a mere thirty years later the population bore very little resemblance to that recorded by H.M.S. *Finder*.

It was a confident, more self-reliant people now, with a conscious bent for independence. From the occasional ships, and a few expeditions of their own, Tanakuatuans had learnt a little of the world outside, and preferred their own ways. Towards chance visitors they were rarely hostile, for they liked barter and enjoyed an opportunity for a feast, but towards those Englishmen, Frenchmen, Germans and others who came to look at the island with calculating eyes, and sometimes made exploratory suggestions upon the wisdom, in this uncertain world, of entrusting the protection of one's interests to a benevolent strong power, their manner was cold and their hospitality formal. It was a matter in which the views of successive chiefs and of their subjects were at one.

On several occasions they came nearer to 'protection' than they ever knew, but each time the old reasons prevented it from actually taking place. Even with the coming of steamers, prospective exploiters continued to decide that the island, in its remoteness, was too small, and its population too unco-operative, for any venture there to be better than a poor risk. And so, though by margins that were at times very narrow, Tanakuatuan independence survived even the Wonderful Century.

But the world was changing. Half way round the globe from Tanakuatua an old Queen died. She had lived under an imperial sun in its high noon, and seen her subjects dapple the map with red patches, from continental daubs to little stipple spots in distant oceans, but when she went that sun, too, was sinking. The shadows of history were creeping over a great day done. Already a new wind was blowing gusty warnings, gathering strength for the gale that would tatter the Age of Confidence to its last shreds. And when that storm came, not even Tanakuatua, twelve thousand miles from its centre, remained untouched.

In 1916 it occurred to someone in the Admiralty that Tanakuatua and Oahomu both stood a good chance of attracting German attention as bases, or hiding places, suitable for their armed merchant-ship raiders engaged in harassing shipping in the western Pacific. This thought he communicated to the Colonial Office with the suggestion that it might be a useful idea to forestall any such intention.

As a result, the Governor of the Midsummers in due course received instructions to take preventive action there. This led him to dispatch the *Frances Williams*, an inter-island trader now equipped for the times with a resplendent coat of dazzle-paint and a quick-firing gun, to show the flag. Her arrival at Tanakuatua, after a reassuring call at Oahomu, took place on the 15th September.

As she entered the lagoon after negotiating the passage of the reef, the Captain lowered his glasses, and passed them to the mate.

' 'Few ask me, Joe,' he said. 'There's something gorn a bit orf here. Been here afore a couple of times, an' each time they all come out on the beach an' start jumpin' up and down an yellin' their heads orf. But just take a shufti now.'

The mate swept the glasses along the shore line. He could see no sign of movement. But for the row of canoes drawn up on the beach the place might have been deserted.

The *Frances Williams* lost her way, and her chain rattled out.

The sound echoed across the lagoon, without rousing response of any kind. Then the mate said:

'Ah. There's two or three of 'em, Cap'n. Keeping well back in the trees. Seem to be wavin' at us.'

As the Captain took his glasses back and turned them where the mate was pointing, four dusky figures broke from cover further along the beach and sprinted towards the water. Almost without pausing, they grabbed one of the drawn-up canoes, and took it with them. They were aboard it and paddling furiously in a matter of seconds. Then, before they had covered more than twenty yards, came the sound of a rifle shot. The bullet fell short of the canoe, throwing up a spurt of water. The paddlers hesitated briefly, and then bent to it again. There was the crack of a second shot. One paddler sprang to his feet. By the time the sound of his howl reached the *Frances Williams*, the canoe had already overturned, and its crew was striking out for the shore.

The Captain ordered the gun-crew to stations, and none too soon. A fusillade of shots broke out on the shore, but the range was long. A few bullets pattered against the ship's side, most fell short. A small gun of some kind opened up with a couple of ranging shots, and then put one neatly through the funnel. The *Frances Williams*' quick-firer replied.

The battle of Tanakuatua was brief. Since the ship's gun had hitherto fired only three or four rounds in practice, and none in anger, there may have been an element of beginner's luck in its marksmanship, but after it had spoken thrice the shore gun was not heard again, and presently a white flag was seen to wave above the bushes close to its position.

Firing ceased. The Captain ordered the boat lowered. The military warrant officer aboard embarked his party, and cast off. Before the boat had covered half the distance there were renewed sounds of rifle fire ashore. Since no bullets came near the boat, it was deducible that the Tanakuatuans, in either contempt for, or non-recognition of, the white flag, had launched an operation of their own. And, it turned out, with some success, for when the landing-party reached the scene they found only four men in German uniforms hemmed into a tight group still defending themselves. The rest of the platoon that had been landed two weeks before as an occupying force was dead.

The Tanakuatuans were delighted.

For one thing, though they had many songs and dances extolling the ferocity, valour, and fortitude of their warriors, these heroes were not, in fact the warriors of the moment, and some fifty years without actual battle experience may have caused them feelings of uncertainty. Thus, to have tradition so notably vindicated, at a cost to themselves of only five or six casualties, gave them an exhilarating sense of being men as good as their grandfathers.

Moreover, they had taken a strong dislike to the German garrison party.

The platoon had landed uninvited on their island, neglecting all proper greetings and formalities. It had then proceeded to erect its tents upon a handy open space – which happened to be clear only because it was a burial-ground. It had fired shots over the heads of a party of elders as they had approached to lodge a protest at the desecration. Thereafter, it had demanded to be supplied with fruit and vegetables, with no suggestions of payment; commandeered a number of young women, irrespective of whether they happened to be wives, or not – also without offers of compensation; killed, rather slowly as a warning to the rest, a young man who had tried to steal one of its rifles; and in general revealed itself as being composed of ill-mannered, offensive persons.

The victory, however, more than compensated the Tanakuatuans for the damage the Germans had done to their pride; it restored their good opinion of themselves. The perfection of the memorable day was spoiled for them only by the warrant officer's insistence that his men should remove the bodies of the German casualties – a measure he proceeded resolutely to carry out in disregard of all protest that by immemorial custom the only seemly way to deal with a vanquished enemy was to eat him.

Tanakuatua was then formally declared to have been annexed to the administrative territory of the Midsummer Isles, and thus to be under the protection of His Most Gracious Majesty King George the Fifth.

It cannot be said that the Tanakuatuans ever showed any enthusiasm for their changed status, nor any awareness of their relationship to the great family of nations of which, they were assured, they now formed a part. They did, it is true, get along better with the new garrison than they had with the Germans. But they did not disguise their pleasure a couple of years later when, after the cause of the whole disturbance had been settled by a lot of talkers on the other side of the world in a place they had never heard of, the garrison was withdrawn.

With that, island life could become normal once more. Almost the only things that prevented it reverting literally to the status *quo ante bellum* were the existence of an Agent who was rarely seen, and troubled no one very much when he did come, and, at lengthy intervals, a ceremonial visit from the Governor himself.

On the latter occasions the Tanakuatuans played up tactfully. There was a formal feast followed by a dancing display, in the visitor's honour. The Governor then responded with a speech of thanks and good wishes, mentioning a day, not too far distant now, he trusted, when it should become administratively possible for the inhabitants of this favoured island to enjoy the same educational and medical facilities which, it was hoped, would shortly be organized on the main islands of the Group. Meanwhile, they could rest assured that he, and, through him, the Colonial Office, were ever mindful of the best interests of this loyal and noble people.

Thereafter, he would be escorted back to his ship by a small fleet of canoes, saluted with shouts and raised paddles, and depart, not to be seen again for another three or four years.

Thus, another generation passed peacefully, with little interruption.

Then, once again, there was a garrison on the island. This time it was more numerous, better armed, and stayed longer. But it was also better behaved, and kept better supplied.

Major Catterman, the Commanding Officer, made a point from the first of treating the Tanakuatuans as the true owners of the island upon which force of circumstances had temporarily placed him. He took the trouble to learn something of their language, attempted to understand their customs, and did his best to respect their ways. His men were strictly forbidden to scrounge. All taros, coconuts, breadfruit, young women, potatoes, et cetera, had to be paid for; so that the islanders acquired a taste for baked beans, bully beef, and chocolate. He even ran a series of elementary classes with the purpose of disseminating some idea of the world beyond the seas. If with this, as with certain other of his projects, there was a discrepancy between intention and achievement, he nevertheless maintained a remarkably harmonious relationship throughout his garrison term.

The C.O., for his part, thoroughly enjoyed his stay. There are only a fortunate few whom the currents of war carry into quiet, congenial backwaters, and he was grateful to be among them. By degrees, he came to think that he had probably been quite a loss to the Colonial Service. But even the ravel of war gets knitted, in time. The guns fell silent; the Japanese went home; Tanakuatua no longer needed protection.

There was a farewell feast with four kinds of baked fish, sliced and flaked taro, roast sucking-pigs, breadfruit fritters, crabs in coconut sauce, curried sea-slugs, prawns in lime-juice, purple sea-snail soup, mango with syrup and coconut cream, bowls of salads, and also rum, which it would have been wasteful for the garrison to take away with them.

The brown beauties of Tanakuatua danced and sang. The young men danced too. With oiled skins and bone ornaments gleaming in the light of fire and torches they performed a ferocious re-enactment of the great victory of 1916. The Commanding Officer, half-stifled by leis of frangipani, and the Chief Tatake happy with good rum and pride in his people, sat with their arms on one another's shoulders and swore perpetual brotherhood.

On the following night the island was the islanders' own once more.

Thereafter, for the next three years nothing much happened except a visit from a new Governor, undertaken to introduce himself to his furthest-flung charges. There was the usual ceremony and an address in which he assured them that they must not think themselves forgotten out here in the ocean. The King was always mindful of their interests and had them very much at heart. In fact, and in due course when the disorganization caused by the war had been tidied up – and that, he was glad to tell them, would not be very long now – they would be able to enjoy all the benefits of education and a medical service to which their loyalty to King and Commonwealth during the years of peril so richly entitled them.

After the customary ceremonies he sailed away. It was thought that, like his predecessor, he might be expected to look in again in two or three years' time.

To everyone's surprise he was back within a few weeks. This time to deliver a very different message.

Something, something cataclysmic, he informed the islanders was about to happen. This thing would take place away out in the open sea to the east. Up out of the ocean there would come a great ball of fire, brighter than a hundred suns together, and so hot that even many miles away the bark would be burnt from trees, the skin scorched off men and animals, and the eyes of anyone who saw it, shrivelled up.

It was improbable that the island of Tanakuatua would be harmed in such ways for the fireball would be far away, *but after* the fireball had flared and died it would leave poison-dust in the sky. This dust would bring an agonizing death to all on whom it fell.

It was hoped, and might very well be so, that none of this dust would ever reach Tanakuatua. If, at the time when the great fireburst took place, the wind were to be blowing from the west, and if it should continue to blow from the west for several days, the island would escape unharmed . . .

But no one could control the winds. A man might judge, within limits, how and where they were *likely* to blow at certain seasons, but nobody could be sure that they would do so. Still less could anyone be *sure* that they would continue to blow steadily in one direction for several days. Moreover, everyone had seen clouds that seemed to move against the wind, showing that while it blew one way on the ground it could be blowing another way high up in the sky. Nothing in nature was more capricious than the wind . . .

Wherefore, the King, concerned as always for the welfare of his loyal subjects, had given orders that the inhabitants of Tanakuatua and of Oahomu, too, should, for their own safety, be removed for a short time from their islands to a place where there was no chance of the death-dust falling upon them. He had further decreed that compensation would be paid to them for any

35

losses of crops or property. The evacuation of Tanakuatua by every man, woman, and child of its people would therefore take place in exactly one month's time.

To the relief of the Governor, who had foreseen long hours of obstinate argument, the pronouncement was received quietly. It did not occur to him that the islanders were too stunned and incredulous to believe they had heard aright.

They were still bemused when the Governor, with a final injunction to make the best of the time granted them for their preparations, re-embarked and sailed off to Oahomu to deliver the same message.

In the evening Tatake called a council of his Elders. The main body of the meeting did not have a great deal to contribute. The older men were vaguely uneasy, but still too bemused to appreciate the reality of the crisis. Consequently the floor was shared almost exclusively between the Chief and Nokiki, the head medicine-man, both operating from hastily prepared positions which they consolidated as the debate developed.

The stands taken by both were clear from the start, however.

'This interference is outrageous and intolerable,' proclaimed Nokiki. 'We must call upon our young men to fight.'

To which Tatake replied flatly:

'The young men will not fight.'

Nokiki challenged him:

'The young men are warriors, the descendants of warriors. They are not afraid of death. They will wish to fight – to fight, and score a great victory, as their fathers did,' he said, and backed this up with a brief, if somewhat biased account of the glorious battle of 1916, as evidence that it could be done.

Tatake explained that no one doubted the valour of the young men; it was good sense that was in question. Everyone had seen the recently departed garrison at shooting practice. What chance had even the most valorous of warriors against rifles and machine guns? The young men would all be slain, to no purpose. Worse than that, the islanders would be weakened, for what future is there for a people that has no young men? A weak people had no rights. The better course would be to stay their hands and preserve their strength in order that their voices should carry weight.

The stronger they remained, the better placed they would be to press for an early return to Tanakuatua when this mysterious cataclysm should be over.

Nokiki gushed scorn. He did not believe in this cataclysm, nor did he accept the talk about a return to Tanakuatua. The whole thing was all lies. A blatant stratagem. This King that the Governors talked about, and no one had ever seen – who was he? The truth of the matter was that the Governor coveted their island for his own purposes, so he had schemed to throw the rightful owners out, and then steal it. It was as simple as that. They were being told to hand over their land, their homes, the bones of their ancestors who had won it for them as a present to the Governor. Better far to lie dead on Tanakuatua than to live as cowards in exile.

Tatake spoke of the compensation and the terms offered for re-settlement.

Nokiki spat.

Tatake proclaimed responsibility for the lives of his people. He would not see them thrown away in a futile battle, nor let them be sacrificed in useless defiance of the death-dust.

Nokiki spat again. The death-dust was a myth. A tale invented for the purpose of frightening them out of their homeland. In all legend there was no such threat as this death-dust – lava, cinders, and ash from smoking mountains, yes – but nothing about death-dust. The expectation that they should believe this bogey story for children was an affront in itself. Chief Tatake might be timorously concerned for the lives of the people, but he, Nokiki, put their honour higher. It was for this honour, entrusted to them all by their fathers, and their fathers' fathers, and *their* fathers before them, that he was concerned. Tatake, he said, spoke of life, but what sort of a life was it that must be dragged out amid the contempt of the ghosts of their ancestors? And with the knowledge, too, that when their time came to die Nakaa would bar their way to the Land of Shades and fling their unworthy ghosts into the pit of stakes where they would writhe, impaled for all eternity. Better, far better, to die now, and join the ancestors in the land beyond the western sea, with honour.

As the debate wore on, each disputant gained greater certainty of his own conviction, and hammered the palisade of his position more firmly home. Comments came from the elders of the Council only rarely. For the most part they behaved as a silent chorus, turning their heads from one speaker to the other, nodding sagely from time to time in bewildered support of each.

The light waned. The blood-red sun sank into the sea. The sky was pierced with spear-tips of polished steel. The rising moon set carbon shadows creeping. And still, far into the night, the great debate went on . . .

There was no civil war on Tanakuatua, though only Nokiki's realization that a waste of warriors now would mean fewer of them to meet the real enemy later on, restrained him from declaring a kind of jehad. He could see nothing in the course Tatake had chosen but decadence and the betrayal of hallowed traditions. Yet, though the temptation to defend the right was strong, his need to conserve his forces was stronger, and he decided with reluctance to postpone the punishment of sacrilege until the pale men should have been dealt with.

The month of grace passed in an uneasy truce between the factions. Roughly three-quarters of the population stood by their Chief, the rest rallied to Nokiki. The discrepancy in numbers, however, was largely offset by the inclusion in the smaller group of most of the young men, and nearly all the fervour.

Thus, though with a certain amount of side-swapping as minds swayed, the matter rode; and thus it was still riding when the Governor returned, this time in a far larger vessel, to preside over the exodus.

He was gratified to find the Tanakuatuans prepared. The two landing-craft were able to run ashore close to the spot where Tatake with his people, and their household goods, and their canoes piled high with fishing nets, and their bales and bundles roped in matting, and the last crops from their gardens, and their squealing pigs tethered by one hind leg, stood glumly awaiting them.

The Governor stepped briskly ashore, greeting the Chief affably. He was agreeably surprised to find the inhabitants of this off-the-map island, with their longstanding reputation for being 'difficult', taking it so calmly. He did not know, nor would he ever know, that without the efforts of the wartime garrison's commander to reach a better understanding with the people and teach them something of the facts of life in the outer world, and more particularly his influence over the Chief, the non-cooperation figure would most likely have been close to a hundred per cent.

As things were, he was able to look round approvingly. (He did not, in fact, approve of much that the islanders intended to take with them. Privately he included the whole lot of it under the comprehensive term 'cag', but tact, he had impressed upon himself, must be the watchword for the day.) He nodded:

'Good work, Chief Tatake. Fine bit of organization. No reason why we shouldn't start loading at once, eh?'

The people stood staring at the landing-craft. The men aboard called to them encouragingly. There was a long, long moment of hesitation. Tatake said something gently in the island dialect. Reluctantly they began to gather their possessions and carry them aboard.

Tatake, unspeaking, almost unmoving, watched while the craft shuttled between ship and shore. When the job was three-quarters done the Governor strolled over.

'Gone very smoothly, eh? Had the roll called, Chief? Made quite sure everyone's here?'

'Nokiki not here,' Tatake told him.

'He ought to be. Where is he? Send someone to tell him.'

'Nokiki not come. He swear it,' said Tatake, dropping into his own language, he added: 'Nokiki has eighty of my people with him. They will stay on Tanakuatua. They swear it.'

'Eighty!' exclaimed the Governer. 'Why didn't you tell me this before? They *must* leave. *Everyone* must leave. I thought you understood that.'

Tatake eyed him dully. He shrugged his big shoulders.

'Nokiki fight. Men fight,' he said. And he looked near to regret that he was not with them.

The Governor clicked his tongue impatiently.

'Lot of damned nonsense. Don't know why you couldn't tell me right away. You mean they defied your orders?'

Tatake looked blank. The Governor said impatiently.

'You say Nokiki come. He not come?'

Tatake nodded.

'Nokiki say fight.'

'Nonsense,' repeated the Governor. 'The order was clear. If they don't come, they'll have to be fetched.'

It had been thought desirable to make as little show of force as possible, but the likelihood of some such situation developing had not been overlooked. The Governor conferred with his officers. Presently, one of his younger aides detached himself from the group and made his way up the beach towards the village. Close to the first hut he stopped and surveyed the empty scene. Then he raised a loudhailer, and, in a dialect close enough to the islanders' own, spoke persuasively to the surrounding trees and bushes. At the end of a two-minute address he lowered the hailer, and awaited a response.

It came. Its form was a spear from an unseen source which struck the ground a yard to his left, and stood there quivering. The young man regarded it with disapproval. He appeared to consider trying more persuasion, and to decide against it. Then he turned, and began to walk back, with carefully unhurried steps. Another spear buried its point a foot behind him.

The Governor scribbled a note, and sent it back to the ship with the landing-craft. Ten minutes later the landing-craft returned bearing an armed and helmeted squad of police. The sergeant in charge spoke for a few moments with the Governor and with the Chief, then, with his men holding their weapons at the ready, moved up the beach and was soon out of sight among the bushes.

Ten minutes or so after they had disappeared the sound of the hailer was heard briefly again. It was followed by an outbreak of shooting; rifles and sub-machine-guns together giving an impressive burst of fire-power. In due course the platoon reappeared escorting forty or so disarmed and frightened-looking islanders. The noise of a group of small arms at close range, and the sensation of bullets ripping leaves and branches to pieces close above one's head had not been at all what the legend of the glorious victory of 1916 had led them to expect.

The platoon, having handed over its sheepish captives, reformed and went back into the woods to look for more. A number of young women began to drift out of the trees in twos and threes to join the discouraged warriors.

Tatake made a count, and reported that Nokiki probably had no more than twenty supporters with him now.

This time, the platoon pushing inland by a path behind the village, ran into an ambush. The trap was sprung a little too early to be entirely successful. The three leading men were speared before they had time to throw the tear-gas bombs they were holding ready, but their companions threw theirs with precision – and that was, in effect, the end of Tanakuatuan resistance. The police returned to the beach once more with another fifteen lachrymose and woe-begone captives who carried one policeman dead, and two nastily wounded. Nokiki was not among them.

The Governor was angry. He turned to Tatake. For a moment he had it in mind to say what he thought of a Chief who could not control his own people. Wisely he forbore. Instead, he asked sharply:

'Not more than half a dozen of them left now, Chief?'

Tatake nodded.

The Governor, too, gave a curt nod.

'Very well. They've had their warning. I'm not going to risk any more of my men's lives just to save a few stubborn oafs. They'll have to take their chance.' He turned to board the landing-craft.

Half an hour later, with the passage of the reef safely accomplished, and the Tanakuatuans wistfully crowding the rails, the ship's engines switched to full ahead . . .

From the shade of a group of calophyllum trees set on a headland the remnant of the resistance party watched the ship swing round in a wide arc, and then dwindle away towards the north-west.

When she had shrunk to a speck, the rank and file of the group, three men and one woman, grew restless, uncomfortably aware that it was a long time since they had eaten. Presently they slipped quietly away.

Nokiki was unaware of them, present or absent.

Soon there was not even a speck: nothing but the wide, empty ocean.

The birds fell silent. The light went swiftly as the sun dipped.

Fireflies started to flitter among the bushes. The moon rose with a path that trembled like a band of quicksilver set in the water. Still Nokiki sat motionless.

His dark eyes were fixed now on the horizon-point of the moon-path, but they did not see it; the pictures in his mind came from faraway places and long-ago tales. He was seeing the great fleets of canoes and the floating villages of huts that had borne his ancestors over thousands of miles of ocean. He was remembering the names of the islands where they had paused for a few years, for a generation, for two or three generations, until the young men and women had grown restive again, and set out once more on the eternal search for paradise.

He was seeing their great war canoes. Craft that would sweep to a beach with the force of fifty paddles to spill out warriors who carried all before them. The names of the victories, and of the heroes who had won them, were commemorated by dances and in songs that rang in the head of every boy as he grew to manhood. They ran in Nokiki's head now . . .

That was his people's way of life. So it had been ever since Nakaa expelled men and women from the happy land: wandering across the ocean, fighting, travelling on again, searching eternally for the lost paradise.

Even the coming of the white men had made little difference to that way of life to begin with – but later, and soon, with increasing swiftness, they had changed the whole world. With the power of their weapons they had annexed territories as they chose – and the people who lived in them too. And from that they had gone on to impose their own laws, setting them above tradition, and their own prudish God above the old gods.

Shamefully, people had given in to this. Protests had been feeble and few. Most people had listened to the white men, and become confused by foreign standards. They had allowed their own customs to be derided and brushed away, neglected their observances, lost respect for their totems. Was it a matter for wonder that the offended spirits of their ancestors should have cast them off in disgust and contempt?

Gradually it became clear to Nokiki that it was with the capture of Tanakuatua that the deterioration of his own people had set in. They had arrived there in the traditional style of their migrations, and in their traditional manner they had swept ashore to conquer the island with their usual valour. But that, he saw now, was the last time it would happen: the end of an era . . .

For one thing since the white man had come and re-ordered the world the old way of life had become impossible. But, worse than that, he sensed an evil in Tanakuatua; an influence which had devitalized his people's spirit.

Gradually the valour and the virtue had dwindled in them. Only once since they had come there had it flared up briefly to bring them the famous victory of 1916. Thereafter it had withered away again until, little by little, they had been reduced to the craven, timorous creatures he had watched being herded away to the ship today.

The last spark of pride had died. The valour of their ancestors had been spent in vain, their famous victories counted not at all, the voices of their ghosts were unheard, their descendants had surrendered in utter ignominy. It was the end.

The moonlight glistened on Nokiki's cheeks. It shone on tears of shame and helpless anger: tears of requiem for heroes dead in vain, for a people in decay, for honour in desuetude, for a world that had vanished forever . . .

In the morning the other four returned. The three men sat down silently at a respectful distance. The woman came close, offering him food on a leaf mat, and water in a carved coconut shell.

Soon after the sun was up all five of them went back to the empty village together. Nokiki was already wearing his finest bone ornaments in his ears and his nose. Now he stood like a statue in his hut while the woman painted his body red and white with the traditional patterns of the tribe. Last of all she drew in red on his chest the spider totem of his clan. When that had been done he put on his necklace of shark's teeth, his chain of turtleshell, his strings of beads and threaded shells, and worked a carved comb into his hair. Finally he fastened on his beadwork belt, and pushed the sheath of a long knife into it. Then he strode out of the hut, and led the way towards the twin hills.

Midway along the linking saddle he selected a spot, and marked it with a white stone.

'Here,' he told the men, 'we will build an altar.' Then he turned to the woman. 'Woman,' he said, 'go now to the Tree of Death, and weave me a mat of its leaves.'

She looked steadily into his face for some seconds, then she bowed her head to him, and went away. The four men set about collecting stones.

The altar was finished by noon, and they rested. Then Nokiki marked out a plot the size of a grave in front of the altar. There he began to dig. He would not let the others help him, so, presently, they went off to find food.

When the woman returned Nokiki had finished his work. She looked at it, and then at him. He said nothing. She unrolled the mat she had woven out of pandanus leaves, and laid it beside the open grave.

Soon after it was dark the four lay down to sleep, but Nokiki did not sleep. He sat as he had sat the night before, looking out over the ocean, seeing again the great rafts, the floating huts, and the war canoes carrying generation after generation on their intrepid odyssey; watching them turn into ghosts, and then into nothingness ...

While the sky was still grey Nokiki got up. He went to the altar, and laid offerings on it. Then he sat back on his haunches, facing across the altar and the open grave beyond it to the east, waiting for the coming of Au, god of the Rising Sun.

As the first rays lit the high clouds Nokiki began to chant. His voice woke the others, they stirred, sat up, and watched.

The chant finished. Nokiki stood up, extending both arms to the first small arc of the sun, praying aloud for the blessing of Au, and, through him, of the other gods upon what their servant was about to do. He paused as if listening for an answer, then he nodded twice, and began on the work.

In the name of Au, and all lesser gods, he cursed the island of Tanakuatua for the ruin of his people. He cursed it from north to south, and from east to west, from the tops of its twin hills to the edge of its low tide. He cursed its soil and its rocks; its hot springs and its cold springs; its fruits and its trees; all that ran or crawled on it; everything that jumped on it, or flew over it; the roots in its soil, the life in its rock-pools. He cursed it by day, and he cursed it by night; in the dry season, and in the rainy season, in storm, and in calm.

His audience had never heard so comprehensive a curse, and it frightened them greatly.

But Nokiki had not done yet. He appealed above Au to Nakaa himself, Nakaa, the lawgiver, the judge before whom every man and woman must pass as he leaves this world for the land of ghosts.

He besought Nakaa to declare the island of Tanakuatua forever tabu to all men; to decree that if men should try to live on it they should sicken and die, and shrivel up so that their dust would blow away on the wind and there would be nothing of them left; and that when the ghosts of such men should come to be judged they might not go on to the Happy Land, but suffer, as all tabu-breakers do, shrieking on the stakes in the Pits for all eternity.

His plea ended, Nokiki stood perfectly still, arms by his sides. He looked the risen sun full in the eye for nearly a minute. Then, suddenly and swiftly, he snatched the knife from his belt, and drove it deep in his chest. He swayed, his knees sagged, and he fell forward across the altar . . .

They wrapped Nokiki in the mat of pandamus leaves, and while the men buried him in the grave he had dug, the woman searched until she found a pointed stone. On it she painted the spider totem of Nokiki's clan, and when the grave had been filled she drove the point of the stone into the trampled earth to mark the place.

The four of them hurried back to the empty village. They paused there only long enough to collect some taros, coconuts, and dried fish, and to fill some gourds with fresh water, before they went on to the beach and launched a canoe.

From time to time as they crossed the lagoon they glanced fearfully back over their shoulders.

There could be no doubt that Nokiki's plea, validated by his sacrifice, would be accepted, but no one could tell how long it would take Nakaa to declare his judgement, nor, consequently the exact moment when the tabu would become law.

Once they were beyond the reef their fears became less acute, and subsided still more as Tanakuatua dropped slowly astern. Nevertheless, it was not until the twin hilltops were below their horizon that the four could relax and feel that they were safely beyond the range of Nokiki's terrible curse . . .

Six months later, the inspection-team which visited Tanakuatua to carry out tests concluded its finding with the summary:

'The foregoing report makes it clear that the shift of wind-direction at ten thousand feet – which occurred two hours after Test Zero, and lasted for approximately three hours – carried some part of fall-out material in a south-westerly direction. The contaminated particles in the course of precipitation were, for the most part, carried back in an easterly direction by the contrary air current at lower level. Consequently, though some contamination did in fact reach the island, as suspected, the precipitation there was extremely light.

'As the figures of counts show, radio-activity is very slightly above normal on the eastern side, but negligible in the rest of the island. Nowhere, however, does it approach a degree within the definition of a dangerous concentration.

'Nevertheless, it is not impossible that an exclusive diet of foodstuffs grown in this even lightly contaminated soil might conceivably produce concentrations cumulatively harmful to growing children. This is highly unlikely, but having regard to the circumstances, and bearing in mind the public reaction which could result from any misadventure even remotely attributable to fallout from this test, it might be unwise at this stage to declare the island officially "clean".

'We would advise against immediate reoccupation of the island, and suggest a further test after an interval of five years. In our view, counts taken then should almost certainly permit classification as completely "clean".'

It was not, in fact, five years later, but nearer ten that the Tanakuatuans, in their reservation, were told that a ship would soon be sent to take them home. The news was not well received. Indeed, such was the outcry that the District Officer paid them a special visit of enquiry.

Tatake acquainted him with the news that the four refugees had brought. The District Officer, though learning now for the first time of the tabu, recognized the seriousness of the situation.

Nevertheless, he felt he could make a suggestion:

'It seems to me,' he said after consideration, 'that, men being as they are, Nakaa must receive many appeals for the imposition of a tabu. It would clearly be impossible for him to grant them all, or there might be so many that life would become too difficult to live. How is it possible, therefore, to know whether he granted Nokiki's request for a tabu on Tanakuatua? What is the evidence that he did not refuse it?'

Tatake shook his head in reproof.

'No man asks lightly for tabu,' he said. 'Tabu is a very serious matter. If he were to ask such a thing from unworthy motives his ghost would be unable to enter the Happy Land, and would suffer for ever in the Pits. Moreover, Nokiki was no ordinary man. He was a devout and honourable man – a great maker of magic. And he surrendered his own life to Nakaa that this thing might be done. Therefore it is clear to us that this thing was done – and is so.

'As in the beginning Nakaa expelled men and women from the Happy Land, forbidding them to return; so he has now forbidden Tanakuatua to all men. '

'This is how you truly believe the matter to stand, O Chief?' asked the District Officer.

Tatake nodded.

'It is.'

'And it is what *all* your people believe?'

Tatake hesitated.

'There are some of the young men who doubt it,' he admitted. 'Since we have been in this place the Christians have got at them. Now they do not believe anything,' he explained.

'Then they, at least, would be willing to return to Tanakuatua?'

The Chief looked doubtful.

'They might, but even without a tabu what would a score or so of young men do there? For no women would go. No,' he went on, 'what they are saying now is that since the tabu cannot be lifted so that we can *all* go back, we should do as our ancestors would have done – find ourselves a new island, and conquer it.'

The District Officer shook his head.

'Times are not what they were, Tatake.'

Tatake nodded sadly.

'But it would be the better way for us,' he said. 'Here my people are slowly rotting.'

The District Officer did not deny it. He asked :

'Isn't there some way – some kind of propitiation, perhaps – of getting the tabu lifted?'

Tatake shrugged.

'That is what some of the young men ask. They do not understand. It comes of hearing Christian talk about forgiving. Nakaa does not forgive. When he has judged, he has judged, and it is forever. Tabu is tabu.'

'I see. Then what do you, Chief Tatake, think should be done?'

'I think it is the Government's fault that this thing has happened to our island. I think, therefore, the Government must give us another island instead – a good island – and help us to move there. We have held councils about this. We have decided that if the Government does not agree to do this for us, we must send a man to the Queen to tell her how her servants have cheated us out of our own island of Tanakuatua, and left us in this place to rot.'

It was an impasse that might have lasted much longer than it did but for the fortuitous visit of a travelling Member of Parliament who was also a gadfly member of the Opposition. During his brief stay in the Midsummers he happened to hear of the Tanakuatuan's complaint, and was much interested, almost to the point of rubbing his hands.

'Ah,' he said, after hearing one or two versions of the situation. 'Very pretty. What it amounts to is that these unfortunate people, who were forcibly removed from their island in the first place because of a bomb test, are still held in a reservation, which they dislike, and the only alternative the Colonial Office offers them is that they should return to that island although the place is known to have suffered contamination from radioactive fallout. Very naturally they refuse to go back there. And who's to blame them? I wouldn't want to be sent back there in the circumstances. And I wouldn't want them sent there, either. Nor would a few million other people if they knew about it ... Good stuff for a Question. Got just about *all* the angles. Very nice indeed.'

The House, however, never heard the Question. The Colonial

Office, by hurried arrangement with the Treasury, bought Tanakuatua from its former inhabitants for a very respectable sum, on paper. With this credit, it then negotiated on their behalf the purchase of the island of Imu. The inhabitants of Imu did not receive a great deal in actual cash, but they did get free transport for themselves and their belongings from their remote island to a generous reservation on a larger and more prosperous island – the very reservation, in fact, which the Tanakuatuans had been occupying for the last ten years.

The solution proved fairly satisfactory all round. It is true that a number of Tatake's more restive young men continued to point out that had the Government not taken their island from them by guile and force the tabu would never have come into existence, but most of his people were disposed to accept it fatalistically as an act of the gods, and prepared to make the best of things on Imu, which was, at least, an island of their own, and not a mere reservation among strangers.

Nor was the Colonial Office displeased with the solution. An awkward Question had been avoided, and now, as ground landlord of geographically inconvenient Tanakuatua (as well as Oahomu, which it had taken the opportunity to purchase at the same time) it could prevent resettlement there. Thus, since they were now uninhabited, it was able to contrive their official severance from the Midsummers Group to whose administration they had never been anything but a geographically inconvenient nuisance.

Thereafter, for a dozen years Tanakuatua reverted to the state of being an almost unvisited dot on the map, forlorn and near forgotten. The taro patches had long gone back to the wild. The coconut palms and the breadfruit trees gradually deteriorated amid choking thickets. The huts of the village collapsed and rotted away until they were overgrown without trace. Almost the only survivals of civilized times were the descendants of a few escaped goats and pigs, free now to live unthwarted lives.

Things could quite easily have been different, however. The multi-sided requirements of science, particularly military science, which may lead to anything from the building of a townlet amid eternal ice to putting a man on the moon, or from cossetting a new virus to herding flocks of electrons, produced a demand for an island. This, though pleasantly inexpensive when compared with the requirements of certain other projects, was more than a matter of allocating funds, for it was stipulated that the island should, among other qualities, be equable in climate, uninhabited, easily patrolled, and well isolated.

The list of available islands, never long, was soon reduced to two, and only the shape of Oahomu, which made its coast line easier to watch and to reach at any point in an emergency, determined that it should be fenced with barbed wire and forbidding notices, and officially designated as a Tracking Station, while Tanakuatua was allowed to drowse quietly on beneath its thickening thickets.

And so it might have remained for many more years had not Walter Tirrie, searching for a suitable location for Lord Foxfield's Enlightened State Project, chanced to hear of it and had himself flown there to look it over.

The island appealed to him at once by its manageable size, its location, and its climate.

He was not equipped to force his way along the overgrown tracks and make a close survey, but he took soil samples in the area of the lagoon where his plane put down, and photographs of the crowding vegetation as evidence of fertility. Unfortunately more photographs taken in a rapid inspection from the air failed to come out, but they would not in any case have been good since, he reported, much of the east side of the island was obscured by mist or low cloud at the time. He was, however, able to see that there was no lack of vigorous growth anywhere save on the upper slopes of the twin hills and the saddle joining them. Even the inside walls of the two craters were clothed with bushes. Several streams, in addition to the hot spring, looked capable of giving an adequate supply of water.

The place would certainly need a lot of reclamation, but that was no obstacle. In climate, in its location far from steamer tracks, as well as in size, it seemed to him ideally suited for our purpose.

Walter's inspection was perforce hurried, and he does seem to have felt some astonishment at finding so habitable an island unoccupied and available. Further inquiries at Uijanji explained that entirely to his satisfaction. In fact, in the recommendation he tendered on his return he included the existence of the tabu, and its deterrent effect on visits by unwanted strangers, as an additional asset.

He duly, when it had been determined which of the Offices of State concerned was the veritable holder of the title to Tanakuatua, made an offer – subject to the production of a certificate stating that all traces of abnormal radio-activity had subsided to an extent warranting the official declaration of 'clean' – of £20,000 for the island.

The certificate was produced, and negotiations took place.

In due course, the representatives of the Crown, knowing nothing at that stage of Lord Foxfield's interest, emerged from them not displeased with their success in conveying to Walter Tirrie, Esq. the title to that unprofitable and troublesome parcel of real estate, the Island of Tanakuatua, in the sum of £30,000.

# Three

An account of our journey to Tanakuatua would be tedious, if only because it went so smoothly, in both senses.

Almost the only unexpected event was, as I have mentioned, the defection of Horace Tupple at Panama. How Horace came to be among us at all is still a mystery. I can only imagine that Walter, in a misguided moment, thought he would act as a kind of leaven. He did not. The poor response that met his attempts to enliven the voyage, and give it a cruise-like quality, with deck-games tournaments, facetious competitions, bingo sessions and the like, together with the atmosphere of our evening discussions – which I admit had something of the style of earnest seminars – had convinced him by the time we were halfway across the Atlantic that he had landed himself in the wrong crowd. Gloom began to dampen his spirits, and his attempts to throw it off became less frequent until the night before we reached Colon he got drunk enough, and uninhibited enough, to give us his opinion of us, and of the Project as a whole. The next day he walked off.

Poor Horace. Lucky Horace!

For my part I set myself to get to know my companions. It was the best decision I could have made. For the first time since my accident I became aware of others, concerned with them as people rather than as numbers, or simply as material for the Project. I had a sense of re-awakening slowly, coming back to life – and, I confess, of increasing astonishment to find myself committed as I was. It was a sensation not exactly of disillusion, but certainly of revelation. A gradual supplanting of fantasy by fact. A slow realization that the Project was no longer theory; that we were, incredibly, on our way to make it a reality. The sense of waking up was both puzzling and a little alarming. It had in some degree that sense of misgiving, of uneasiness about what one may have done, that I imagine to follow a loss of memory.

It was fortunate, I have since thought, that the process was gradual. It would have been truly alarming had it been sudden.

As it was I felt my companions changing little by little from figures into living people – and into different people from those I had expected them to be. And, perhaps, too, now we were on our way, they *did* change to some extent . . . All I can be sure of is that *I* changed, and that I saw them differently. Doctors used to be in the habit of recommending a cruise for various malaises; it could be that they had something there. Certainly it cleared my mind, and with consequences that were not altogether reassuring.

It came, for instance, as a disconcerting discovery that it brought home to me that the provision of means and opportunity had not produced identical opinions on the ways to employ them. I seemed in my earlier, or lyric, phase to have been thinking with the naïvety of an early socialist that all must love the highest rationality when they saw it. I began to percieve, as if for the first time, that rationality is not a constant – it varies subject to individual concerns and the pressures of personality – and as a consequence that our progress towards the formation of an ideal community might be less smooth and less selfless than I had envisaged.

In fact, I became aware of my faculty of judgement stirring again, as if from hibernation.

One of its effects was to make me increasingly conscious of the very general, not to say sketchy, nature of some of our intentions. The more I thought of the way we had taken the co-operation of everyone for granted, and failed to make provision for the settlement of disagreements, the more uneasy I became. I perceived the need of an authority for reference, established by consent and available for matters in dispute, as offering greater stability than *ad hoc* settlements.

My efforts to pin Walter down to discussion of these, and other details which now seemed to me to have been left vague, were unsuccessful. He took an empirical line regarding such matters, brushing my approaches aside with the assertion that a formal attitude, too cut and dried, would lack the flexibility to adapt itself to circumstances. It was out of our circumstances and conditions that our institution must grow, he maintained, and refused to be drawn into argument.

This, coming from a planner of his ability, puzzled me considerably, but unable to make any headway against it I gave up after three or four attempts. Indeed, it was not the only thing about Walter that I found unexpected. He was, in general, less approachable than he had been during the preliminary work. His manner had altered, and he spent a great deal of his time in his cabin. In fact, it was not long before I had the impression that he was progressively holding aloof from the rest of us; slowly building an intangible barrier round himself – and not only round himself; it partially included Alicia Hardy who appeared to be taking on the manner of his confidential secretary.

To the rest, I suppose, the change in him was less noticeable than it was to me who had worked with him. For most of them he was the organizer, and, as such could be expected to have plenty on his mind. Of them all, only Charles Brinkley noticed the withdrawal enough to mention it, and then only in passing.

As the voyage wore on I set myself to learn more about my companions. It was not difficult. With little to occupy them, they were mostly ready to talk about themselves with very little encouragement.

I learnt without any difficulty Charles's views on the restrictions that hedged around farming in England, and how, in exasperation, he had sold up a good farm in Nottinghamshire in order to take a chance on virgin land where he could grow crops as he saw fit, without interference and without spending half his time on paperwork.

I learnt of Joe Shuttleshaw's disagreements with a number of his bosses, his union, and the class system, and how he wanted his children to grow up in a society which had none of these things.

I learnt of various disillusions that had caused Tom Conning and Jeremy Brandon to get away from it all; of the frustration that had impelled Jennifer Deeds; the romanticism which had suddenly decided the other Jennifer; the idealism which filled David Kamp. In fact I could attach reasons, real or ostensible, to almost all the company.

Some of them were not convincing. Camilla Cogent, when I joined her at the rail one day before we left the Atlantic, showed no disposition to confide her reasons, in fact, she had kept herself apart and apparently far away. It was her isolation that prompted me to approach her and attempt to draw her in – that, and something about her that reminded me of my daughter, Mary. When I asked her why she had come, she continued to look unseeingly at the water for so long that I thought she had not heard me. Then as I was about to repeat the question, she turned to me, still with her faraway look, and said in a flat voice:

'I thought I might be useful. Besides, as a biologist, the idea of an island that has been uninhabited for twenty years fascinates me.'

With that for the time being I had to remain content. It enabled me only to decide that her real reason was another negative – something she was getting away from. It occurred to me then that we were remarkably short on positive incentives, and I was thrown back on my previous reflection about only the misfits being free.

Nevertheless, Camilla, too, changed as the voyage went on. She discovered interests in common with Charles. The two of them would discuss problems of propagation and breeding by the hour. Mrs Brinkley set herself to bring Camilla out in her kindly way, and with some success. The faraway look, though frequent, was no longer constant.

We fell into routines. Charles doing his miles per day round the deck to keep himself fit. Jennifer Deeds conducting her daily classes for the Brinkley and Shuttleshaw children – which they all appeared to enjoy. Mrs Brinkley ensconced in deck-chair comfortably turning out unending knitting and chatting amiably to anyone who joined her. Jeremy Brandon and Tom Conning alternately beating one another at deck-tennis. Marilyn Slaight flirting with one man after another, apparently for the satisfaction of making it up with her husband after a fine row between them. And so on.

It was not until one afternoon in mid-Pacific that I exchanged more than a few polite words from time to time with Camilla. The others who had been under the canvas awning at the stern had drifted off, leaving us in sole occupation. I was reading, Camilla lost in contemplation of the ocean – at least for a time – but when I looked up from turning a page, I found that she had transferred her attention to me, and was regarding me with a slight frown. At least it was an improvement on the faraway look. I inquired:

'Can I help?'

She started to shake her head, and then changed her mind.

'Yes – after all you asked me questions. Do you mind if I ask you some?' And without waiting for an answer she went on, 'You see, I'm puzzled. How did someone like you come to be included in this?'

'That's not difficult to answer,' I told her. 'Basically because I thought it worth doing – or, at least, trying.'

She nodded slowly, her eyes on my face.

'Do you mean thought – or think?' she asked shrewdly.

'I've not given up before it's begun,' I said. 'Have you?'

She did not answer that. Instead, she said;

'What I don't understand is the – well, the amateurishness, to use a kind word. There seems to be plenty of money behind it.'

'There were several possible ways of launching it,' I explained. 'At one time Lord F contemplated the idea of causing a town to be created – rather in the manner of a miniature Brasilia – and made ready to receive the chosen. But the cost would have been prodigious, and even had he been able to stand it there would have been little left over for the endowment, which he considered very important – particularly during the first years. Without a substantial endowment it might never be occupied, and would stand a good chance of becoming the wrong kind of monument – an empty city at the world's end known as Foxfield's Folly.

'Or he could have employed contractors to carry out a less ambitious scheme under the direction of the first settlers. That was feasible, though costly, but he rejected it chiefly on the grounds that it would import an undesirable element which could result in a frontier mining-town atmosphere creating standards and practices that might be very difficult to eradicate later on.

'So it was chiefly his desire not to start off on the wrong foot which decided him to make a modest start with a pioneer party, whose task would be just as much to bring into existence a community with acceptable standards as to create habitable conditions.'

'And this is it,' she said, without any particular inflexion.

'It has been done before. Smaller ships than this took the first settlers to America – and they made at least a material success of it. Their misfortune was the size of the place – which created the need for manpower, any kind of manpower, at any cost to their principles. We don't have to start with the axe, the handsaw, and the spade – we should have a better chance . . .

'Besides,' I went on, 'he thought the construction of a community by the community would have a psychological value. It would be better integrated, work out its own codes and mores, feel pride in what it had constructed, and acquire a sense of solidarity which would equip it to deal unitedly with outside influences that are bound to be felt from time to time.'

She contemplated for a moment.

'Yes, I can see that is sound theoretically, but it scarcely presupposes – well, *us*, does it?'

'I don't know. Most of us are not of the calibre he had in mind,' I admitted, 'but it isn't easy to persuade the most capable, even if they are sympathetic, to throw over their commitments, sell up their homes, and take a chance on a somewhat hazily defined project on the other side of the world. Mostly you have to be content with what you can get. And, after all, we are only the pioneer party. Once we get established and there is something to come to, once the project can be shown to be on its feet, it could well begin to appeal.'

'When I told my father I was coming, he gave it about three years,' she remarked.

'To fail, you mean?'

' "This isn't the first time it's been tried," he said. "After about three or four years, or even less, they usually peter out." '

'If you believe that, why did you come?'

'Because I wanted to get away, and, as I told you, because I thought it would be an interesting place. Why did *you* come?'

I told her. She looked at me consideringly.

'You are still a romantic,' she said, in a wondering way. 'You can still dream dreams.'

'While you, at twenty-six is it, are old and disillusioned?'

'Yes,' she said. Then, after a pause, she added. 'I don't want to believe again. I have been hurt enough. But hope doesn't have to be so committed. One can hope from outside. It would be all the more fascinating to see one's hopes taking form – less painful if they did not.'

'Just a well-wisher?' I suggested.

'And a well-worker, I hope. But faith ... no, I'm not putting that up in the crockery-smashing stall again. "Men like gods" is too tempting a target for the opposition.'

'All right,' I told her. 'Come to think of it, there's many a valuable piece of work done without faith – only it's less rewarding.'

In subsequent conversations I learnt more about her. That she held a D.Sc., and was thus entitled to be called Doctor. (Though she never used the title other than officially, partly because the English have a feeling of masquerade about any doctor who is not a medical man, and partly because she felt it to sit intimidatingly on a woman.) After taking her degree she had worked for some time in a Government Research Laboratory on various branches of pestology. Later, for reasons which she did not specify, she had elected to take up field-work. This had taken her first to West Africa to look into the habits and lifecycle of yet another menace to the cocoa crop there; then, to an island of the Chagos Archipelago in the Indian Ocean to investigate a form of blight which was affecting the breadfruit trees – both the true *Antocarpus Incisa* and, oddly enough, the *Encephalartos Caffer* too, she explained. Following that, she had spent a year at home, about which she said nothing. Now, I gather, she was looking forward to seeing what interesting pests and blights might have developed on an island left twenty years in isolation.

Talking to her, I began to understand why, in spite of her dubiety about the success of the Project, Walter had taken her on. When she talked on her own subject the faraway look disappeared altogether, and one was left with little doubt of her knowledge and capability.

Our last port of call was Uijanji (We-yan-ye), the capital, and the only port in the Midsummers. We stayed there a couple of days, and when we sailed took on board a party of some twenty Islanders recruited locally to help with the landing of our supplies on Tanakuatua.

Camilla was surprised that they had been willing to come. She had spent the time at Uijanji ashore, finding out all she could about Tanakuatua, both generally, and in her own field. It had given her plenty to think about.

'From what I've heard, the place is under a very comprehensive curse indeed,' she told me. 'Any native who is willing to risk setting foot in the place must either be very sophisticated – or very sure of some kind of protection.'

'Or possibly decadent?' I suggested.

'I included that under "sophisticated",' she replied. 'It will be interesting to see how far they've managed to outgrow the primitive when we actually get there.'

Two days later we arrived.

At first sight Tanakuatua was like romantic tourist literature come to life. Photographs had prepared me for the shape of it, but not for the colour. That was dazzling. The blue of the sky, enhanced by scattered white clouds, was reflected in the shifting blues and greens of the sea. The island was a slash across the middle to separate them. A line of white beach, a vivid band of green above it, and beyond, the expected shape of the twin hills, but now green for two thirds of their height, and blue-brown for the rest. My first feeling was of disbelief that such a gem of an island could have been left deserted. My second, a twinge of misgiving: it looked too good to be true.

We made the passage of the reef without difficulty, and moved slowly across the lagoon. Then the engines went astern. Presently the anchor chain rattled through the hawse-pipe, shattering the silence and echoing back and forth across the lagoon. A few birds rose from the islets in the reef, and circled with harsh cries.

Camilla, at the rail beside me, looked at them, and then back towards the shore. She frowned, and murmured, more to herself than to me:

'Strange, so few birds ... I'd have expected thousands of birds ...'

The work of getting ashore began.

Soon after we left Uijanji, a derrick had begun hoisting parcels of nested containers from the hold, and dumping them on the deck. The first job now was to separate them, fix an airtight lid on each, and drop it over the side. There, the Islanders, swimming as if water were their native element, manoeuvred them together, and joined them by links on their sides. The result, in a surprisingly short space of time, was a large, articulated, very buoyant raft.

Walter deserves full credit for the idea, for the quite astonishing numbers of cases, drums, bales, bags, and bundles that the hold now began to disgorge would have needed innumerable boat trips to get them ashore, and several of the larger crates could not have been handled by that method at all.

In a couple of hours or so the loaded raft, towed by a fibre-glass boat with a powerful outboard engine, began to move slowly away from the ship's side. Those of us left on board raised a scattered cheer, and waved down to those on the raft.

The stately progress must have taken almost half an hour before the raft actually touched the shore, and then as it did, an entirely unexpected thing happened. All the Islanders who had crowded to its forepart leapt off, splashed through the shallow water, and ran up the beach. We could see Walter and Charles, left on the raft, waving to them to come back, but they took not the least notice. They kept on running without a backward glance until, just short of the bordering trees, one of those in the lead stopped, and raised his arm. The rest stopped, too, and formed a semi-circle around him.

The leader spoke, paused, then made a gesture with his hand. They all went down on their knees, arms upstretched, then, at another sign, they bent forward and remained, faces to the sand, in an attitude of supplication. Presently the man in the middle got to his feet again, raised his arms, and stood motionless. His face was turned inland, his back towards us, so that it was impossible to see whether he was speaking or not.

Through the glasses one could see Walter and Charles in argument, still aboard the raft. It was evident that Walter wanted to go after the Islanders. Charles, with a hand on his arm was dissuading him – and successfully, for after a few moments Walter shrugged, and resigned himself to wait.

Beside me, on deck, Charles' son Peter inquired of Jennifer Deeds:

'What are they doing that for, Jenny?'

'I don't know,' she admitted. 'People have different ways in different places. Perhaps they think it's the polite thing to do when you arrive on an island.' After a pause she added: 'It rather looks as if it might be some kind of propitiation ceremony.'

'What's a proppy – what you said?' Peter asked.

'Oh, dear. Well, you see, simple people think the world is inhabited by lots of spirits, as well as by men and women,' she explained. 'So it might be that they are afraid that the spirits here won't like us landing on their island uninvited. So I wouldn't be surprised if they are praying to the island spirits not to be annoyed with them – and perhaps asking their permission to stay for a day or two. It's a bit like – well, like the way some people touch wood just to be on the safe side; only we don't take that sort of thing very seriously any more, and these people do.'

'He's turned round. Now he's making a speech to them,' Peter said.

He appeared to be doing just that, and at some length. After that he, too, prostrated himself again, with the rest. Several times the whole party rose upright on its knees, and went down again.

'Could well be,' I agreed. 'From the little I've read a tabu-breaker has need of all the spiritual sanction he can get. Let's hope they feel satisfied that they've got it. If not, I can see us with a strike on our hands, and a lot of heavy work to be done.'

Apparently they were. The ceremony, whatever it was, lasted about twenty minutes, and then broke up. The Islanders drifted down the beach back to the raft, and began unloading as if there had been no interlude.

Charles Brinkley acted as beachmaster, supervising the construction and arrangement of dumps, and organizing the stacking of conveniently sized cases in such a way that they could be covered with canvas sheets to make sleeping quarters until the pre-fabricated huts should be assembled.

Mrs Brinkley, too, revealed herself as a capable organizer and efficiently directed the construction of a field kitchen. Jamie McIngoe supervised the layout of the machinery and constructional materials dump, and got one tractor uncrated to move the larger cases. The rest of us did as instructed to the best of our ability as long as the light lasted. Then we returned on the raft to the *Susannah Dingley*.

After dinner I went out on deck where I presently discovered Camilla regarding the island's black bulk by the light of innumerable stars and a rising moon.

On the foredeck the Islanders were holding a kind of singsong. A single voice alternated with choruses. The voice would chant or declaim to the accompaniment or rhythm strummed out on a tumpy-sounding drum, then the rest would join in. The choruses were not repetitive; sometimes the song would be plaintive with the quality of a lament; occasionally it would be louder and hold an undoubtable tone of triumph; once or twice it was simply a cheerful tune; but it was the note of lamentation that predominated. After each song the rhythm of the drum would change again and the single voice would take up its saga. I wished I could understand the tale it was telling.

We listened in silence until it came to an end, and the voices broke into chatter.

Camilla nodded her head towards the island.

'Well, what do you think of it?' she asked. 'Is it what you expected?'

'It's beautiful,' I said. 'But it's intimidating. So much growth – with so much vigour. All those plants fighting one another for existence. And we've got to fight them. A great neglected tangle that will have to be cleared by sheer hard work – and then kept clear.'

'More raw than you thought?'

'Yes, I suppose so – insofar as I did think. I don't remember going into details. In fact I've rather skipped over the beginnings. I've tended to see it in later stages.'

She glanced at me.

'Ah, yes. A kind of Arcady. A wide, rolling, tree-dotted scene with flocks of sheep grazing on Downs turf watched by contented, pipe-playing shepherds, with, here and there, a small city, all white, severe and beautiful.'

'Come, come,' I said. 'My romanticism is at least this century's.'

'I'd not be too sure of that,' she replied. 'And anyway, one of the troubles of this century is that people have learnt to patronize Nature. That's perhaps preferable to the last century's guff about Mother Nature, but it's just as unrealistic. It probably does one good to be brought up against the facts of life now and then – at least it makes one realize that there is a struggle going on; that you have to do more than wave a cheque-book to create "men like gods".'

I wasn't going to argue about men like gods. I asked her:

'How do *you* find it? Is it what *you* expected?'

'Yes, I think so. Mind you I've only been a few yards from the landing-place, so far. The secondary growth is perhaps a little denser than I'd looked for, but generally speaking it *is* much what one had expected. Except for the birds ... I don't understand that. There ought to be millions of birds ...' She paused, considering. 'There seem to be fewer flowers, too – still, that could be due to a number of causes. Might be purely local.'

'Apart from that it's much as you'd expect to find a place without any men to upset the balance of nature?' I suggested.

She did not reply immediately. Then she said:

'If I were given to thinking in phrases of that kind, I'd not be in my job.'

I was puzzled for a moment until I perceived what she must mean.

'The balance of nature? That's a common enough expression, surely?'

'It's common, as you say – and mischievous.'

'I don't see why. After all, we've been upsetting it enough to change half the world in the last generation or two.'

She said, patiently:

'It is mischievous because it is ill-considered, and entirely misleading. To begin with, the idea that man *can* upset what you call the balance of nature is a piece of arrogance. It assumes him to be outside the natural processes – the "man like god" theme again. Man is a product of nature – its most advanced and influential specimen perhaps, but evoked by a natural process. He is part of that process. Whatever he does, it must be part of his nature to do – or he could not do it. He is not, and cannot be, *un*natural. He, with his capacities, is as much the product of nature as were the dinosaurs with theirs. He is an *instrument* of natural processes.

'Secondly, there is no such thing as the "balance of nature". It does not exist, and never did. It is a myth. An offshoot of the desire for stability – of the attempt to reduce the world to a tidy, static, and therefore comprehensible and predictable place. It is part of the conception of a divinely appointed order in which everything had its place and purpose – and every man had *his* place and task. The idea of natural balances goes right back to the origins of magic – left balanced by right, white by black, good by evil, the heavenly host by the legions of Satan. It was an article of faith set out in the Zohar that "unbalanced forces perish in the void". The attempt to reduce an apparently chaotic world to order, of a kind, by the conception of balanced forces has gone on since earliest history – and it still goes on. Our minds look for reasons because reason, and balance, give us the illusion of stability – and in the thought of underlying stability there is comfort. The search for stability is the most constant – and the most fruitless, quest of all.'

I was taken aback. I had evidently trodden on a tender corn, or at least introduced a hobby-horse for her to ride. I did not care for her lecturing manner, particularly from one young enough to be my daughter, but she had not finished yet. She went on:

'Nature is a process, not a state – a continuous process. A striving to keep alive. No species has a *right* to exist; it simply has the ability, or the inability. It survives by matching its fecundity against the forces that threaten it with destruction. It may appear for a time to have struck a balance, a fluctuating balance, but it has not. All the time there is a change – change of competitors, change of environment, change of evolution – and sooner or later any species will prove inadequate, and be superseded.

'The reptiles after dominating the world for millions of years were superseded by the mammals. The mammals have recently been dominated by the super-mammal, man. And yet people talk glibly about "preserving the balance of nature". It is impossible – and if it were possible, why should it not have been the Mesozoic "balance" of the giant reptiles just as much as any other period that stood in need of "preservation"? Why should the existing state be so much more valuable than the past – or the future?'

'Surely,' I said, taking my opportunity to break in, 'surely the crux of the present concern is the improved methods of destruction – insecticides, and so on, and the inability to determine the side-effects of their use. Isn't it due to the speed of everything nowadays? – when you can exterminate a species in a year or so, and only begin to perceive the secondary effects when it is too late? It seems to me that is another way to the dustbowl.'

'It could be,' she agreed. 'But the discretion in their use needs to be intelligent, not sentimental. Behind most of this talk of "balance" I perceive the old idea that "Mother Nature" knows best. Leave everything to her, don't interfere, and she'll look after us. Which is, of course, complete rubbish. It is a concept that could only have arisen in a comfortable, well-fed society which has forgotten what it is to struggle for existence. Nature is *not* motherly, she is red in tooth and claw, she ravens for food – and she has no favourites. For the time being we are sitting pretty – but not for long. The same laws that operate for every species that outbreeds its food supply will operate for us. When that happens we shall hear no more of this benevolent Mother Nature. Without the knowledge we have of manipulating Nature for our own ends our present population would already be going hungry – if, indeed, it had come into existence at all. The only difference between us and other species is that we have superior equipment for preying on them, and for coercing Nature for our own benefit. Beyond that the same rules apply. There is no warrant whatever for supposing one can "preserve the balance of nature" – with man comfortably in the saddle, which is what the whole concept implies.'

We looked across the water to the dark bulk of the island.

'Well,' I said, 'if one takes a long enough view, I suppose all existence can look futile. A planet is born, it cools, it brings forth life, it dies. So what?'

'So what, indeed?' she replied. 'There is only the life-force, the patriotism of species. And that is blind. It is shared by the highest organisms and the lowliest . . . and understood by neither . . .'

'How do you, speaking as a biologist, see the future of man?'

'I can't look round corners. Life is full of accidents and imponderables. He seems evolutionarily to have come to an end. But he is not effete. Who can tell? He *may* produce a new type – and *may* allow it to survive. He may all but wipe himself out, again and again – and start again each time, becoming a new creature in the process. Or he may be superseded . . . just scrapped; another of Nature's unsuccessful experiments. On the face of it, and as he is at present, I can't see much future for him.'

'No men like gods, in fact. And not much prospect for this project.'

'Oh, I don't know. As you said, things move so fast nowadays, and, as I said, there are the imponderables – so there's time for a number of unexpected discoveries in the next two or three thousand years. I only said that in his present condition and state of knowledge there doesn't seem to be much future for him. One discovery – in the field of controlled heredity, for instance – could alter the whole outlook.'

'Well,' I said, 'let's hope. Let's even go so far as to hope that Lord F's Project is a success – and that it is here that the discovery may one day be made.'

'You do really believe in it, don't you?' she remarked.

'I believe in it as a possibility. All things have small beginnings. Nationalism is becoming too narrow, too restrictive. The advanced men are beginning to feel the need of a place where they can live and work, and exchange ideas without restrictions. Someday they are going to make such a place for themselves – a kind of mind powerhouse, as Lord F said. Set on its feet, given time, this *could* be the place. Why not?'

She looked across the water for some moments, without speaking. Then:

'It's a wonderful vision,' she admitted, 'but it's before its time. I can't see the world tolerating it.'

'Possibly you're right. But I think it's worth trying. A kind of world university, the mecca of all the talents – and if it fails this time, well, at least there will be lessons to be learned from its failure, and the next time, or the time after that, it will be successful.

'His lordship may be a vain man, even rather a silly man, but the idea is bigger than he knows. After all, if it should succeed, and one day come to hold the reins of knowledge it will be a power. It will have authority. As a unifying force it might succeed where the League of Nations failed, and the United Nations is failing.'

'You are a romantic – and in a big way,' she said.

'Perhaps,' I admitted, 'but unification must come in one way or another – or else destruction. The democratic way doesn't appear to work; it's not the United Nations that prevents destruction breaking loose now; it's the balance of power. Perhaps an autocracy – an autocracy of knowledge – might work better . . .'

We talked on for an hour or more. The young moon rose higher, silvering the sea, turning the island from a dark mass to a shimmering shape which seemed to float on the water. I forgot the emptiness of it, the neglect, the choking vegetation. In my mind's eye I saw it in order; planted, cultivated, cut by wide roads, set with fine buildings where unimaginable discoveries were being made. It was a brave sight – alas for it . . .

# Four

The quantity of our stores and supplies laid out on the beach was prodigious. It took all of us working from dawn till dusk five days to get it all there, but it was done at last. We said good-bye to the skipper and crew of the *Susannah Dingley*, watched her edge her way carefully through the passage of the reef, heard her give a couple of triumphant toots on her hooter, then saw her turn to the north-west and start to dwindle. It was to be six months before she returned with more supplies and, we hoped, more personnel for the project. Until then we were on our own.

It was remarkable how palpable that feeling of being on our own became. As long as the ship had been anchored in the lagoon we were linked with the outside world, but as she disappeared below the horizon the sense of isolation closed in. Everybody, even the children, felt it. We found ourselves looking at one another speculatively as if seeing ourselves afresh, with the reality of the situation only now coming home to us.

For myself I felt more than isolation. I felt that the island was no longer a neutral neglected place waiting for someone to put it in order. It seemed to have undergone a change; to have become no longer a passive, but an active, challenge. To have taken on an air of resistance, even hostility. I found myself wondering whether that was the result of knowing it to be taken, of that knowledge working in the primitive, subconscious part of my mind to arouse the ancient fear of a curse ... It was quite ridiculous, of course. For a curse to be effective one must believe in its efficacy, which I certainly did not. And yet I had the feeling that the island was brooding – inimically ...

Whether some of the others had the same sensation I don't know, but the departure of the ship left us all in a subdued mood, and it was Charles who took steps to break it up.

He and Walter had already chosen the site for the settlement, drawn up plans for it, and started staking the positions for the huts. Now he called us together, led us to the site and explained how it was going to be laid out. His confidence was infectious. Before long he had all of us visualizing how it would be, and asking questions. Within half an hour the oppressive sense of isolation had lifted, and everyone's spirits appeared to rise. We trooped back to our temporary quarters – and to Mrs Brinkley's cookhouse – feeling encouraged and capable.

During the meal Walter composed two messages to be dispatched via our radio to Uijanji for onward transmission. The first was to Lord Foxfield. It announced the successful completion of the landing operation, the departure of the *Susannah Dingley*, and that the work of turning the Project into a reality would start tomorrow. The second, for publication and circulation among our relatives and friends, assured them that we were all well, and in good spirits.

When they had been read out and approved, he handed them to Henry Slaight who took them away for transmission. In a couple of minutes Henry was back, with a look of concern on his face. He bent down and whispered to Walter who got up and left with him. I slipped away and followed them to the nook among our stacks of cases which formed the temporary radio office. I found them peering inside by the light of a battery lamp. Over their shoulders I could see that where the transmitter had stood on a folding table there was now a wooden packing-case. The table, and the transmitter, were crushed beneath it.

It was a heavy case, and it took our united strength to move it aside. One glance at the transmitter was enough. It could be written off. We all turned to look at the gap in the top row of the wall of cases immediately above. It was evidently where the case had come from, but:

'It can't just have fallen . . .' Walter said.

He tested the stability of the stacked cases with his hand. They stood rock firm.

'It's impossible,' he added, uneasily.

We looked at one another. Walter shook his head.

'But who –? It must have taken two or three men to dislodge

that . . .' He shook his head again. 'Better say nothing at present. Let them think the messages have gone off. I'll break it to them later.'

The next day work began in earnest. Charles got the bulldozer going, and took it off to start clearing the site. Tom Conning started ferrying materials to it with the tractor and trailer. Henry Slaight strung lights through our temporary quarters, and got the generator uncrated to provide power. Mrs Brinkley chose her cookhouse squad, and got them busy. Jamie McIngoe went off, prospecting a pipeline route for a water supply. Joe Shuttleshaw with a gang of helpers began sorting out the parts of sectional buildings, and stacking them ready to be moved up as required. Jeremy Brandon put the concrete-mixer together and made it ready. Everybody, including the children, was found a job of some kind.

It went on like that for six days – leaving us all dead tired at the end of each. But we had something to show for it. By that time Charles had the central site cleared, and had started on preparing more land for cultivation. Much of the clearance debris had been gathered into piles and burnt. The foundations for the first building, a communal dining-cum-general-hall with kitchens attached, had been poured, and the parts of it lay ready for erection. The concrete-mixer had moved on to prepare more foundations, these for a storehouse in which our more vulnerable supplies could be got safely under cover. Jamie had run a temporary pipeline to our camp, and had started digging a trench to take a permanent one to the site. Altogether we were not displeased with our progress, and felt we had earned the rest day that Walter declared.

The question was how to spend it. Tom Conning, however, had no doubts.

'It's time we saw something of the place. It's nearly a fortnight since we landed, and so far nobody's been more than a quarter of a mile from here. I propose to climb the mountain – if you can call it a mountain, at any rate it should be high enough to give a view of the whole island. Anyone come with me?'

Alicia Hardy and four of the younger ones promptly accepted the invitation. Joe Shuttleshaw's boy Andrew held up a hand, too. His father pulled it down for him, and he protested loudly. Tom said:

'Let him come, Joe. He'll be no trouble.'

I looked at Camilla.

'Not you? I thought you were getting impatient to see more of the place.'

'After the last week I'm not spending my rest day hacking my way along overgrown tracks. I've looked at them. I doubt whether they'll get halfway in a day. Besides, you can't see anything when you're occupied with slashing. I've got a more comfortable idea. If Walter will let me have the boat we could go round the coast, and perhaps land here and there.'

She got the boat. Walter was half-inclined to come in it himself, but Charles persuaded him to stay and work on some modification of their plans. Most of the others seemed to be content to take the rest day literally. They proposed to do nothing more energetic than lie in the shade, and recover from the energies of the week.

So, the following morning, after we had seen the exploring party, all armed with machetes, make their start, we launched the boat and set off.

There were five of us aboard: Camilla, Jennifer Deeds, David Kamp, Jamie McIngoe, and myself. Since we had already seen something of the western coast from the deck of the ship as we approached, we decided to go south, round the southernmost point and make our way up the east coast.

There was a set-back when we discovered that the reef did not continue round the island as we had supposed. Instead, it swept in to join the southern headland, so that we found ourselves in a cul-de-sac, and we had to follow the reef half a mile back before we found a safe passage to the open sea. Fortunately it was a calm day with only a light wind, and a gentle swell running.

We turned eastward again, keeping well off the reef but passing the south cape inside the islet of Hinuati, which lies something under a mile off shore.

On the far side of the cape the coastline changed entirely. Instead of the white beaches we found low basalt cliffs standing sometimes with their feet in the water, here and there separated from it by a narrow strand of greyish sand, and shouldered at intervals by falls of boulders that projected into the sea. They stretched away to the north like an irregular wall, sometimes sixty feet high, sometimes a mere twenty-five, but seemingly without a break. The sombre, forbidding aspect of them was made the more cheerless by the lack of movement, except for the waves splashing at the cliff-foot nothing moved.

I heard Camilla ask herself in a puzzled tone:

'But *why* are there no birds . . .?'

'God,' said David, 'what a coast to be wrecked on.'

We chugged on in a subdued mood.

Then I noticed something else. Up on the cliff top the vegetation crowded to the very edge. Nearby, the bushes and the tops of trees were quite sharp and clear, but further away they became hazy, and in the distance it was as if the whole cliff top were fringed with a dingy white.

'What on earth's that?' I asked.

Camilla shook her head. 'It could be some sort of blight,' she suggested.

Jennifer Deeds put in: 'I seem to remember Walter mentioning patches of mist on the eastern side when he flew over it to inspect.'

'Aye, he did so,' said Jamie McIngoe. 'Maybe it would look like that from above, but that's no mist.'

Nobody contradicted him. Apart from the fact that the light breeze would have dispersed any mist, it looked too static. Camilla produced a pair of field-glasses and studied the cliff-tops as well as she could against the slight rocking of the boat. Presently she lowered them.

'I don't know. It doesn't seem to move at all. It must be a blight of some kind. Can't we go a little closer in?'

I borrowed the glasses off her. It was impossible to keep them trained on one spot, but I could catch glimpses of the outlines of leaves and branches through the stuff that shrouded them on the nearer trees, further away it seemed to grow more opaque and to lie on them like a bank of soiled snow. But what it was I could form no guess.

Jamie cautiously edged the boat nearer to the shore as we went on, but we could not make anything of the stuff, only that it was certainly more solid than the first we had seen. Looking at it through the glasses now one caught occasional iridescent flashes.

'I must get some of that stuff and examine it,' Camilla said.

'You'll need to be a good climber,' David told her, looking at the cliffs.

'There must be a break somewhere. Will you put in, Jamie, when we find one?' she asked.

We went on. About half a mile further along we found a break – of a sort. It was a small bay about fifty yards across. The cliffs here were no more than thirty-five feet high. In the middle they were split by a cleft down which flowed a small stream. The sides of the cleft looked scarcely more climbable than the face of the cliff itself, but the stream had evidently carried down silt so that at the foot of the cleft a bank had formed some feet above the high-tide level. There a number of bushes and small trees had taken root and formed a clump. Hiding the top of them was a cloud of the mysterious static mist.

'We'd be able to reach that,' said Camilla. 'Can we land here, Jamie?'

Jamie scanned the shore line of grey sand fringing the bay. He grunted, doubtfully, but he swung the nose towards the shore, reduced speed, and began to approach cautiously. David went forward and hung over the bow, shading his eyes, to peer down through the clear water.

'Sandy bottom,' he reported presently. 'Looks all clear.'

Jamie reduced speed still further, and held one hand on the reverse lever, ready to throw it immediately. There turned out to be no need. David kept on reporting clear sandy bottom until we were close in. The beach here shelved gently. Jamie gave a final spurt, and as the bow grated on the sand, he shut off the engine.

The silence came down like a blanket. It had such an unnatural, ominous quality that for some moments none of us moved. We sat there looking at the dark cliffs, and the dreary grey sand of the beach stretching smooth and unbroken except by half a dozen patches of brownish stuff which looked like clumps of stranded seaweed.

'Not a welcoming spot,' said David.

'It's like the dead end of the world,' Jennifer said. Then she gave a little exclamation.

'Look!' she said, pointing to the nearest clump of seaweed. 'It's moving!'

We looked. The brown patch was irregular in shape, looking as if it had been spilt there. The main part of it measured about two feet by three feet. There was no doubt about its motion. It was sliding slowly across the beach in our direction. At that distance we could make out no details. It suggested something seen under a low-powered microscope, an enormous amoeba flowing across the sand.

'What is it? I don't like it,' Jennifer said nervously.

David laughed. He jumped out of the boat and started to splash his way through the few yards of water that separated us from the dry sand. Almost immediately the brown patch speeded up, coming down the beach towards him, at almost walking pace, elongating slightly as it came.

David stopped to watch it, bending forward a little. Then he laughed again, ran forward and jumped over it, and went on running up the beach towards the bushes.

The brown patch stopped, then went into reverse, and started to follow him.

'Look,' cried Jennifer, 'the other ones, too. Look out, David!' she called.

All the other half dozen patches on the beach were now in motion, converging towards him at walking pace. He looked round and saw them. He paused to wave a reassuring hand to us, and then ran on, jumping over another of the patches that was advancing ahead of him. It, too, altered direction to follow him.

We saw him reach the bushes and jump up to grab some of the misty stuff that covered them.

It was impossible to be sure what happened then. One moment he was completely visible, the next something seemed to fall on him, half-hiding him.

Then there was a scream. While it was still echoing across the little bay, David turned and came pelting down the beach towards us. His head and shoulders were turned to a brown blur by the stuff that had fallen on him. He kept on at full tilt to the water's edge and into the water, until he tripped and fell with a great splash a few feet away from us.

Jamie and I leapt out of the boat to go to his help. As we waded towards him we saw the brown stuff coming off him, resolving into hundreds of globules and washing away. We paid no attention to it. We laid hold of him and turned him over. I had a glimpse of his face, a vivid scarlet, as we dragged him back to the boat and lifted him aboard with the help of the two women. Then we climbed aboard ourselves, and stood panting from our efforts while Jennifer examined him as he lay in the bottom of the boat.

Presently she looked up. In a wondering, incredulous voice she said:

'He's dead. David's dead.'

Unnoticed by the rest of us Camilla had climbed over the side. She returned in time to hear Jennifer's verdict, carrying something wrapped in a handkerchief. This she put carefully in a corner of one of the seats before she climbed up and turned to look at him.

'Yes. He's dead,' she confirmed, and continued to examine the vivid face with great attention.

Jennifer turned away.

'If you hadn't been so keen to know what that misty stuff is ...' she began, and left the sentence unfinished.

'If David hadn't gone to find out, we might all be like that,' Camilla replied.

She looked across the beach. Most of the brown patches had become static, though one or two still drifted slowly and aimlessly back from the water's edge.

Jamie turned his attention to the engine.

'We'd best take him back,' he said, and pressed the starter.

Camilla sat looking at the cliffs and the mist-topped trees that crowned them, with a frown of concentration as we drew off. The frown was still there when we were in the open sea, making our way back down the coast. I offered her a cigarette. She took it and lit it absent-mindedly. Not until she had finished it and thrown the end over the side did she break her thoughts. Then it was to say:

'I don't understand – I simply don't understand it.'

'We ought to be able to get a specimen some way or other,' I said.

She looked at me blankly.

'A specimen of the misty stuff,' I explained.

'Oh, *that*,' she said.

'Well, I thought that was what you wanted . . .'

'Oh, I know what that is.'

'What is it?'

'It's a web – just spiders' web.'

I turned and looked at the coast. At the misty white tegument that covered the trees. I boggled at the thought.

'But that's impossible. All that web. It'd take billions, quadrillions of spiders . . . No, I can't believe it . . . It's inconceivable . . .'

'Nevertheless, it's true,' she said. She reached down beside her, picked up the rolled handkerchief and unfastened it carefully.

'There they are. They're the cause of it,' she told me.

I looked at the contents of the handkerchief. Half a dozen spiders, all with their legs clenched tightly about them in death. With a finger she turned one over so that I could see its back.

It was not a large spider – certainly not for what the tropics can show. The body was just about an inch long. The marking was a pattern of dark brown on a ground of russet brown. It looked a very harmless creature.

I raised my eyes to the cliff-top again, and shook my head. 'I can't believe it,' I repeated.

'That's what's done it – unless there's another kind, too,' Camilla assured me. 'Certainly this is what got David.'

I stared at the thing. I had heard of poisonous spiders, of course, but I had imagined them to be large, hairy-legged creatures, far larger than this. I still could not believe it.

'What sort of spider is it?' I asked her.

She shrugged.

'They're rather a specialized study. It is an adult, female. Class: Arachnida. Order: Araneae. Sub-order: Araneomorphae. In other words it is a true spider.'

'So I judged,' I said.

'I can't say more,' she told me. 'I daresay it has a name. But as there are six hundred kinds of spiders in England alone, and heaven knows how many kinds in these parts, positive identification is asking a bit much. It needs a specialist, as I said. All I can tell you is that structurally it appears to be just a normal spider. I'll have a look at it under the microscope when we get back.'

'But it is poisonous? You know that?' I insisted.

'*All* the Araneae are poisonous,' she said. 'Whether they are harmful to us depends on whether they are strong enough to puncture our skins, the nature of the poison they inject, and the quantity of it.'

Jennifer had joined us, and was peering down at the spiders in Camilla's handkerchief with horrified fascination.

'These must be very poisonous indeed – like the black widow or the tarantula,' she said, with a shudder.

'I shouldn't think so – or they'd be just as notorious, even though the tarantula is mostly a myth,' Camilla told her.

'I thought from what you told us that insects and pests *are* your speciality,' Jennifer said.

'They are,' Camilla agreed calmly. 'But spiders aren't insects – though some forms can be pests. The rest are, as I said, out of my field.' She looked down at the dead spiders again. 'All the same I'd guess that a bite from one of these, since they can puncture the skin, might itch and swell a bit – but wouldn't be likely to have much more effect than that.'

'Except that they killed David,' Jennifer said bitterly.

'Exactly. The effect of two or three hundred bites injecting poison at approximately the same time would, of course, be very different. *That's* what I don't understand,' Camilla replied, with a shake of her head.

She unscrewed one of the object-lenses of the field-glasses, and used it to examine one of the spiders more closely. After some moments she said:

'Nothing exotic about it. Eight eyes, strong chelicerae – as you'd expect, to bite through human skin – six spinnerets. In fact, as far as appearance goes, a very ordinary spider indeed.' She continued to look at it, thoughtfully. 'The reason I know so little about spiders is that the Araneae are not pests. If they were, they'd have been studied a lot more than they have. They're seldom harmful, we haven't found any use for them, with the result that only a few specialists have taken much interest in them. In the normal way their lives and ours scarcely impinge. Fortunately they do kill vast quantities of insects which would otherwise become pests, but apart from that we might be living in different worlds. They go their way and we go ours, and mostly we interfere with one another only by accident. Almost perfect co-existence – that's what makes this so strange . . .'

'Insects,' I said, reminded. 'Yes, there aren't many, are there? I expected an island in these parts to be swarming with them.'

'And I expected far more flowers,' Jennifer put in. 'But if there aren't the insects to fertilize them . . .'

'And I am beginning to have a pretty good idea what has happened to the birds,' said Camilla.

# Five

I had hoped to get ashore quietly and ask Walter's or Charles's advice on dealing with David's body, but there turned out to be no chance of that. Several people who were idling around the encampment saw us approaching and came down to greet us, so there was no hiding it. We sent one of them back for a blanket to cover the body, then we carried it up and laid it in one of the bags among the cases. Then Jamie and I went in search of Walter. We discovered him and Charles together in a tent which had been put up at the site to act as an office, at work on a drainage plan. They received our news incredulously, and came to see for themselves.

'Spiders!' exclaimed Walter. 'It's unbelievable. What kind of spiders?'

We explained that Camilla had the specimens. Presently we discovered her under a tarpaulin awning where she had set up a microscope on a table, and was intently examining one of the spiders through it.

'I can't find anything unusual,' she told us. 'It has all the looks of a perfectly normal type – though I can't identify it. There are too many kinds. I'll try to dissect one if I can – it's a very tricky job. But I'll be surprised if there's anything to be found – I mean, abnormally developed poison glands, or anything of that kind. I think it's just the numbers of them that made it fatal.'

'There were a lot of them?' asked Walter.

'They seemed to drop on him in a mass – impossible to say how many,' Camilla said.

'There must have been several hundreds in each of those groups on the beach,' I put in. 'Though of course we didn't know what they were then – they simply looked like moving brown patches.'

'You think there's an infestation of them round there?' Walter asked.

'Infestation is a mild word for it,' Camilla told him. 'You remember those patches of mist you reported seeing?' She reminded him, and went on to tell of the quantities of web we had seen from the sea. 'And we've no idea how far inland it covers,' she concluded.

Walter looked down at the three or four dead spiders lying on the table.

'It seems impossible. I never heard of spiders behaving in such a way,' he said.

'That is what is troubling me,' Camilla told him. 'Spiders definitely *don't* behave like that. There is a class known as hunting spiders, but they certainly don't hunt in packs. In fact, spiders don't do anything in packs . . .'

Walter remained thoughtful for some moments, then an anxious expression came over his face.

'The exploring party hasn't returned yet,' he said, uneasily.

There was still no sign of the exploring party when the sun went down.

An air of apprehension hung over the whole encampment. Joe Shuttleshaw was the most restless. From time to time he would walk along the beach to the point where the party had started hacking its way along one of the overgrown tracks. There he would put his hands to his mouth, and call at the top of his voice. Then he would pause and listen, as we all listened, for an answering call. None came. He'd try again, with no more result. Then he'd trudge back and sit down beside his wife, biting at his fingernails.

'Ought never to have let him go. I told him not to,' he muttered from time to time.

To begin with Charles tried to encourage him.

'Probably went too far. Misjudged the time it would take them to get back. Finding the going difficult in the dark,' he suggested.

But when a couple of hours of darkness had passed he gave that up. We just sat, not talking much. Listening intensely, but less hopefully, each time Joe gave one of his hails.

Three hours after dark Joe came back once more to the fire we were keeping well ablaze as a beacon. He demanded:

'Isn't somebody going to *do* something? My boy's with that lot. Some of you come out and help me look for him.'

He stood gazing round at us. Nobody moved.

'All right, then. I'll go by myself,' he said.

'Oh, no, Joe,' implored his wife.

'Come now, Joe,' Walter said. 'You can't get along through that stuff in the dark. That's very likely what they've found out, and decided to lay up somewhere.'

'You don't believe that, do you?' countered Joe.

'It's what I'm hoping,' Walter told him. 'If I'm wrong, and they have run into danger, there's no sense in any of us running ourselves into the same danger – particularly in the dark. We've got to wait till morning.'

Joe stood there irresolutely, his wife plucking nervously at his sleeve. He glanced again into the darkness. Presently he sat down, staring disconsolately into the fire.

We had kept the news of David's death from the children. Now Chloe, the eldest Brinkley child inquired:

'What's dangerous, Daddy?'

Charles replied diplomatically:

'Walter only said *if* there were any danger, dear. You see, we really don't know very much about the island yet. There may be – er – snakes and things, so it's well to be careful.'

'Oh,' said Chloe. 'I thought you might mean the black men.'

'Now why should you think that?' Charles said, puzzled. 'They were perfectly harmless fellows. Anyway, they all went away home, on the ship.'

'Oh, then they must have been other black men,' said Chloe.

Charles looked at her with more attention.

'What must have been other black men?' he asked.

'The ones Peter and I saw this afternoon,' she told him.

He regarded her for a moment, and then turned inquiringly to his son. Peter nodded.

'Yes,' he said. 'They hadn't any clothes on, and they were all shiny.'

Charles frowned.

'Where was this?'

'We went up to see the buildings, and it was very hot there so we came away and sat in the shade of some trees, and while we were sitting there they came out of the trees further along.'

'How many of them?'

'Only two.'

'What did they do?'

'Nothing. They just stood at the edge of the trees, looking at the buildings, then they disappeared again.'

Walter leaned forward, regarding the two of them intently.

'You're quite sure of this?'

'Oh, yes,' Chloe assured him. 'Peter saw them first. Just the top half of them among the bushes. He pointed, and then I saw them, too.'

Walter looked round the circle.

'Has anyone else seen these men, or any signs of them?'

No one answered. Heads shook.

'They can't have been here when we came. There'd be traces of some sort. Did anyone count the Islander party aboard before they left?'

'One naturally supposed the skipper would have arranged for that,' Charles replied.

There was a reflective silence until Jamie McIngoe put the question which was in everyone's mind:

'If it's some of that lot that have stayed behind, what would they want to be staying for?'

It remained unanswered – and troubling . . .


In the morning we dug a grave, and laid David's body in it. Charles spoke a short prayer over him, and we filled it in.

Of the exploring party there was still no sign.

Joe Shuttleshaw continued to demand a search-party. There were no volunteers. Walter with Charles' support continued to temporize.

'It's no use our going blundering in until we know more about what we're up against. Anything that has accounted for a party of seven – *if* it has, which we don't yet know – can as easily account for another party of seven, or more. The best thing we can do now is to get on with the work.'

There was little enthusiasm for that.

It was Camilla who proposed a solution. She tackled Walter.

'Joe's right,' she told him. 'We can't simply do nothing. There must be a search. I've an idea I'd like to try out. Now, first, have we any insecticide?'

'Several drums of different kinds,' he told her.

'And spray-guns?'

'There should be two or three dozen, but –'

'Good,' she interrupted. 'Then this is what I propose to try . . .'

By midday she and Joe were prepared. Both wore trousers tucked into high boots, long-sleeved jackets fastened to the neck, and gloves. On their heads were wide-brimmed hats, crudely woven out of split cane and palm leaves. Over the hats, disposed in the manner of a bee-keeper's veil and tucked into the jacket, were two or three thicknesses of mosquito-netting. They were carrying machete scabbards attached to their belts, and both were armed with spray-guns which they had already used liberally on each other.

'Not that insecticide is likely to do much harm to spiders,' Camilla said, 'but they've sensitive feet, and they won't like it, so it may keep us free of them.'

They refilled the spray-guns. Joe hung a spare can of insecticide on his belt, and they were ready to start. Before they left Charles beckoned Camilla aside, behind the angle of some of the packing cases he put his hand in his pocket and then extended it towards her.

'Can you use one of these?' he asked her.

She looked at the revolver in his hand.

'Yes, but –' she began.

'Then you'd better take it. After all, we're not *sure* that the spiders are the only trouble, are we? But look after it; we may need it later.'

Camilla hesitated, then:

'All right. Thanks,' she said, and slipped it into her pocket.

We all accompanied them to the start of the overgrown track along which the exploring party had already hacked a path, and watched them make their way up it until they disappeared at a turn. Then we trooped back.

I, for one, was feeling rather small. I imagine Walter was, too. He said, with a slightly defensive air:

'After all, it was her idea . . . And she was right about there having to be a search, of course . . . But we can't afford to risk more people than we have to . . .'

It was four hours later that Camilla returned. She was out of the trees and halfway to us before anyone was aware of her. She was walking slowly, carrying her hat and veil in her hand. We ran to meet her.

'Where's Joe?' Mrs Shuttleshaw cried.

'He's coming,' Camilla told her, with a vague backward gesture.

'Did you find them?' Walter asked.

She looked at him with a blank expression. Then she nodded slowly.

'Yes ... We found them ...' she said.

There could be no doubt what that meant. She was looking all-in. I glanced at Walter, and led her off towards the encampment. He stayed behind to quieten the rest. By the time he joined us, I had her sitting in a chair, drinking a stiff brandy and water.

'They were all dead?' he asked.

She nodded, stared at her glass for a moment, and then finished off the brandy.

'They'd got about a mile and a half,' she said.

'It was the spiders?' asked Walter.

Camilla nodded again.

'Myriads of spiders, swarming all over them.' She shuddered. 'Joe wanted to find his boy. He started using the spray-gun on them. It was horrible. I came away ...'

'They didn't attack you?' Walter asked.

'They tried,' she said. 'They came for us in hundreds, and started to climb up our legs, but they didn't like it. They soon let go and fell off. Some of them dropped on us from the bushes, but they soon fell off, too.' She shook her head. 'They kept on trying. Hundreds of thousands of them. The others can't have had a chance. It must have been quick – like it was with David ...'

There was a sound of voices outside. Walter looked out.

'It's Joe,' he told us, and left.

I went to the entrance. Away near where the track left the shore I could see a figure, carrying something in his arms. Behind me Camilla's voice said:

'I tried to stop him. What's the use ...?'

I poured her another brandy. She looked as if she needed it. Ten minutes later, looking somewhat recovered, she said:

'We'd better join them.'

We found them where we expected. Four men with spades were digging a grave alongside David's. Joe Shuttleshaw was sitting on a fallen tree, a little apart, looking utterly blank. His wife knelt beside him, her arms round him, tears running down her face. He seemed unaware of her. His burden lay on the ground close by, covered with a blanket now. His eyes never left it. The rest stood around, silent and horrified.

Charles said his prayer again – and included in it names of the six others who had been on the exploring party. The sight of Andrew Shuttleshaw's body had altogether banished the idea of sending an expedition to bring the others in. Then we dispersed, most of us in a very thoughtful mood.

It was in the evening that a deputation called on Walter. It consisted of Joe Shuttleshaw, his wife, and Jeremy Brandon, and its purpose was to tender their resignations from the Project. They demanded that a message should be sent to the *Susannah Dingley* calling her back to take them – and anyone else who had changed his mind – off. Calling at Uijanji, as she was scheduled to do, they argued that she could not have got very far away yet. If that were not possible, then Uijanji itself could doubtless provide a smaller boat to get them that far.

Walter, who had been postponing the news about the radio-transmitter was thus forced to lay the whole situation before them. Joe lost his temper, and refused to believe him until he was taken to see the damaged transmitter. After contemplating its undeniable uselessness for some moments, he turned on Walter and more or less accused him of wrecking it himself in order to prevent anyone from walking out on his precious Project.

At this point Charles was called in to give Walter support. He succeeded after a time in bringing the deputation to its senses – or near enough to them for its members to retire and reconsider among themselves.

The following morning, faced by a state of subdued mutiny, Charles called everyone together, and put the situation squarely before us. It was that without means of communication we were on our own for six months. If, when the ship returned, anyone wished to leave, he was at liberty to do so. In the meantime everything would depend on our own efforts. The area of infestation appeared to be no closer than a mile and a half away. There was no telling at what rate it would approach us, or, indeed, that it would approach at all, though it would be wise to assume that it might.

The obvious course, then, was to press on with the erection of the sectional buildings. The sooner they were up, the sooner we should have quarters that could be rendered safe from infestation. Furthermore, our present makeshift arrangements would give us little protection against rain and storms once the weather broke.

Squabbles and recriminations would get us nowhere. We were all together in the same boat. The survival of all depended on the work of each of us. Our setback had been the result of an entirely unexpected condition. Now we knew what the danger was we should no longer be taken by surprise: we could take steps to protect ourselves.

The first step, he suggested, was to create a barrier against the spiders. To do this he proposed to use the bulldozer to clear a perimeter strip some six feet wide which would enclose both our present quarters and the settlement site. At points along this would be spraying apparatus kept ready charged. A patrol would be maintained beyond the strip, and at any sign of the infestation approaching an alarm would be given and the whole length of the strip would be sprayed with insecticide. This, as Camilla had shown, was an effective deterrent and would present the spiders with a barrier they could not cross. That would be our first line of defence, and even if it should not be one hundred per cent effective, the buildings would give us complete security, once they were completed.

He also recommended each of us to contrive for ourselves an outfit such as Camilla and Joe had worn the previous day, and to acquire the habit of wearing it whenever we went outside the perimeter.

Charles, one must say, made a good job of it. He considerably reduced the bogey quality of the spiders, and replaced it with the feeling that they were simply an unusual pest which could be foiled, and most likely overcome, by work and ingenuity. His air of confidence was infectious. We trooped off to work with a greatly improved morale. In the evening Camilla sought me out.

'Hullo,' I said. 'I haven't seen you working. Where've you been all the day?'

'Spider-watching,' she told me. 'I've just had a dressing-down from Walter about it. Not as such,' she added, 'he agrees that the more we know about their habits, the better we'll be able to tackle them. He's annoyed with me for going alone.'

'And very properly,' I agreed. 'It was a ridiculous thing to do. Suppose you'd broken an ankle, or just sprained it. Nobody would have had any idea where to look for you.'

'That's more or less what he said,' she told me. 'I promised I wouldn't go again unaccompanied. But that raises a problem. I suppose you wouldn't care to do escort duty tomorrow?'

I hadn't seen that coming. It took me rather aback. I hesitated.

'Well –' I began.

'It's all right. You don't have to come,' she said.

'No. I'll come,' I decided. 'What do I need?'

'The same kind of outfit as Joe and I wore. Spray-gun. A pair of field-glasses.'

'Very well,' I agreed. 'Now show me how to weave a hat.'

We set off the following morning, carrying our hats and veils until they were needed. For a couple of miles we could keep to the beach, walking just above the water line where the sand was firm, and the going easy. That brought us to the end of the lagoon and the first rocks of the headland. We climbed up them on to the low cliffs. There progress slowed; from time to time, we were held up by the necessity of hacking our way through thickets.

There was no sign of web on the bushes yet, but Camilla considered it wise to put on our veils, and use the sprays on one another.

'As far as I can see at present,' she said, 'the webbed area represents conquered and settled spider territory with an outward pressure of population. Between that and us is a strip of unsettled country prowled over by roving bands of spiders. Troops of pioneers, as it were, gradually pressing forward into new lands, while the territory behind them fills up. One thing we ought to think up is some means of determining their average rate of progress. That would give us an idea of how much time we have to make preparations. Or, whether perhaps we ought to move further north to gain more time before they reach us.'

'That would be difficult,' I told her. 'We're more or less anchored where we are by our supplies. We couldn't move them far from our present position.'

'Probably the best way is to think in terms of defences,' she agreed. 'But it would help to know when to have them ready.'

We emerged from the bushes presently on to a somewhat higher rocky headland. It gave us the best view we had yet had along the coast ahead and of the shoulder of the southernmost of the twin hills, and we sat down and looked at it, filled with awe.

The webbed area began so gradually that it was impossible to determine the edge of it. It started as a tenuous, uncertain haze which about a mile away along the coast ceased to be transparent and became to all appearances a solid sheet, as if the whole tract of land behind the coastline to a level halfway up the hillside had been covered by a fall of slightly yellow snow. Or perhaps the uneven outlines of the shrouded trees made it look more like a cloudfield seen from the air. Here and there it glistered with iridescence in the sunlight . . .

We went on looking at it in silence for a minute or more. My mind felt swamped by the uncountable numbers, the billions of spiders it must represent. It was Camilla who spoke first, and out of a different mood.

'What price the balance of nature?' she observed.

We went on. There was still little or no web on the bushes we passed, but presently we began to encounter packs of spiders hunting on the ground. The first of these I did not perceive until it actually attacked. It came out of the bushes on my left and was around my feet before I realized. I involuntarily jumped aside. Behind me Camilla said: 'It's all right. They won't hurt you.'

She was quite right. They swarmed over my boots, some of them started to run up my legs as far as the knee, but then they abruptly lost interest, dropped off, and scuttled away. Those around my boots soon withdrew, too.

'Spiders smell, or taste, with their feet – and they don't like the stuff a bit,' Camilla said calmly.

I went on with restored confidence. We encountered a dozen

or more such troops but they all retired discouraged. Soon we came out on another headland overlooking a small bay with a beach. I remembered noticing it from the sea, and identified it as the last forest-bounded piece of coast before the line of unbroken cliffs began. The line of bushes with a few trees among them came down to meet the edge of the sand which had already a greyer tinge than that on our side of the island. Dotted about the sand were seven or eight familiar shapeless brown patches.

'Ah,' said Camilla, with satisfaction.

This particular area of the headland appeared to be free of spiders so we sat down, and took out our glasses.

Mine told me little. The groups of spiders were so tightly bunched together that no individuals were discernible and I could see little more than with the naked eye. I tried one group after another, all looked identical, and immobile. I lowered the glasses, and then heard Camilla give an exclamation under her breath. As I was about to follow her line of sight a movement of one of the patches caught my eye. I raised the glasses again and saw it travelling, still as an inseparable unit, on a slant down the beach.

'Something's stirred them,' I said, as I noticed a second patch start to move.

'It's that crab,' said Camilla. 'Look up by the trees.'

I turned my glasses on a black speck there and saw that it was indeed a crab. It was about five feet out from the trees, scuttling down the beach towards the water. Further down, two of the brown patches were flowing along in converging lines to cut him off. The crab swerved, a few seconds later the two patches altered course to intercept him at a different point.

Suddenly the crab stopped, and stood motionless, claws up-raised and ready. The two spider-groups continued on their way, then gradually they slowed up, finally coming to a halt within a couple of feet of one another. The crab started off again on a new slant towards the water. He might have made it, for he appeared to have slightly more speed than the spiders, but by now a third group of the spiders was on the move, converging on this new course. He seemed not to have noticed them until they were close upon him. At the last moment he swerved again but too late. The spider-groups swarmed over him. He managed to run on for a couple of feet, then he slowed, stopped, and was lost to sight under the mass of spiders.

Camilla lowered her glasses.

'Instructive,' she said. 'Their top speed as a group seems to be about four miles an hour. Their sight is bad – as with most spiders. Did you notice – they lost him when he stopped still? They anticipated his line of travel, and aimed to intercept. That's most interesting – it implies that they collectively *knew* he'd be making for the water. And then when he changed course they did, too – after a delay of a few seconds – again to a line of interception. Very curious . . .

'But the amazing thing is that they got him – a crab, armoured all over – and stopped him in a couple of feet. They must have gone for his eyes, of course – and perhaps his limb joints, though one wouldn't think . . .'

She pondered a moment, and then lifted the glasses again, and directed them at a nearer group which she had been watching before the crab incident. We both watched them for some little while in silence. They were not travelling, but neither were they static as the other groups were, indeed they were in a state of continuous activity, much as was the group swarming over the crab.

'Maybe it was just another crab,' I suggested after a time.

It was near to eleven o'clock. After our early start I was feeling hungry. I pulled some sandwiches out of my haversack, and offered her one. We sat there munching, but keeping an eye out for further events on the beach.

The day was warm – too warm for comfort, dressed as we were, but I felt no temptation to remove any of our precautions in an area where a band of spiders might materialize at any moment. The only concession I made was to fold the veil up on to the hat brim, whence it could be dropped again in a split-second. The hat itself I was glad of, for the sunlight poured down strongly from an unclouded sky. I longed for a cooling breeze, but there was scarcely a breath stirring.

Camilla, who had shifted her attention from the bay, to gaze at the great sheet of web further along the coast, gave a sudden exclamation, and grabbed her glasses. What she was looking at I couldn't at first make out. Then I saw a tenuous column rising from the spread of white. One could only make it out against the blue background of the sky, and then so thinly as to be barely certain of it. Camilla tilted her head back, following it up and up. I picked up my glasses, too, I found it, and traces of it going up to a tremendous height, but could make nothing of it. For a moment I wondered whether it might be steam from the hot-spring, but realized almost at once that that would disappear after a hundred feet or so. Then I noticed another vapour-like column rising from further away. This one showed a distinct kink at something over a thousand feet, but went on to climb much higher. A sweep with the glasses revealed three more distant columns, and traces of others that I couldn't be sure of. I lowered the glasses, and looked at the white covering again.

'We must have been wrong about that. It can't be web; it's something evaporating,' I said.

Camilla shook her head.

'It's web all right. What that is,' – she nodded towards the nearest of the columns – 'is emigration. Spiders for export. They've found a thermal, and are going up with it. Millions of baby spiders setting out into the world.'

I said, incredulously: 'Spiders can't fly.'

'Given the right conditions, they can – baby spiders. Web is a wonderful thing. Did you never read *The Voyage of the Beagle*? How they woke one morning more than a hundred miles from land to find the whole deck and the spars covered with little spiders?

'What they do on a nice calm, warm day is to climb to a high point – the top of a tree, or a bush, or even a blade of grass will do – spin out a few inches of silk, and wait. Sooner or later the silk will be caught by a rising thermal and lift them off. Then they go up with the thermal, just as a glider does. It may take them up twenty thousand feet or more. That's what's happening over there.'

I looked at the vaporous columns and tried to imagine it. Millions upon millions of baby spiders launching themselves into space on the chance that the wind would carry them to a new land.

'They'll all come down in the sea,' I said.

'Ninety-nine point nine nine nine per cent of them will,' she agreed, 'but what does that matter with a fecundity like theirs?

Some of them will survive, and breed.' She glanced again at the columns. 'Fortunately they're going high and the direction of the upper air is easterly. That, I imagine, must be the prevailing wind in these conditions, carrying them away from our side, otherwise the whole of the island would have been overrun already.'

As she stopped speaking I caught sight of a movement on the edge of the piece of open ground to our left. Camilla noticed it, too. A troop of spiders emerged from the rough grass, coming towards us. I made to get up, but she stopped me.

'Don't move, and they won't notice us. Remember the crab,' she said, and continued to watch them with a confidence I was far from sharing as they approached.

There must have been three or four hundred in the group. It was the first chance we had had of observing them closely when they were on the move and not actually engaged in an attack. Even so, it was difficult to distinguish individual spiders. They moved with such uniformity, packed so closely together that it was hard to see how they had room to use their legs. Even at close quarters they presented the appearance of flowing along as a single body.

We were sitting directly in their path. Had I been alone I should certainly have got out of their way. Camilla, who was nearer to them than I, simply continued to regard them with interest.

About four inches short of her leg the entire group stopped as one. I was reminded of a well-drilled squad of soldiers coming to a halt. Presumably the leading members had caught a whiff of the insecticide, and found it distasteful. After a momentary pause the whole lot did a left turn and marched on keeping four inches from the leg until the boot was passed. Then they did a right turn, and continued on their interrupted way.

We watched them disappear beneath a low bush on the other side.

'Well, well! A fine, disciplined body of troops,' said Camilla.

She picked up her glasses again, and resumed her study of the beach below, dwelling for some time on the nearest group. It was still active, apparently without purpose. After watching for some minutes she said: 'They're digging. Scooping a hollow.'

I looked, too. She seemed to be right. There was now a sloping bank of sand to one side that I had not seen there before. But what the purpose was I could not make out .There were too many spiders scrambling about the excavation for me to see it clearly. Presently, however, Camilla laid down her glasses, with a sigh.

'Well, well, well!' she said again.

'What is it?' I asked.

'Turtle's eggs. That's what they're after,' she told me, and became thoughtful. Presently she lifted her gaze to the tegumented stretch of forest.

'I wonder what it's like in there?' she murmured. 'They've finished off the birds – presumably the eggs first, and then the birds themselves – they've reduced the insect population close to zero. Presumably they've polished off anything else that walked, or crawled. There can be very little left to eat there now but one another. The survival of the fittest, with a vengeance! They've been driven to hunting the sea margin for food. How long, I wonder, before they learn to catch fish?'

'Or build boats?' I suggested.

'No. I'm perfectly serious. They learnt to build webs in order to catch flying insects. Spider silk is wonderful stuff. It *could* be woven into nets that would catch fish.'

'Oh, come,' I said. 'Think of the strength of a flapping fish.'

'Think of the strength of woven silk or silk cord – it's the same stuff basically.'

She shook her head. 'There's no reason against it – in fact, from what we've seen today it's very likely – it, and a lot of other things ...

'I don't suppose you've grasped the full implications of what we've been seeing. But you can take it from me, revolutionary is a mild word for it. You see, spiders are very old. They've been here for many millions of years. They developed so early that their ancestry was obscure until recently; it seemed as if they had always been here, unchanged and unchanging. They are prolific, but so utterly repetitive that naturalists ignored them. With their origins so far back they held little interest because they seemed to lead nowhere; they had completed their course, a finished species, with no power of evolution left in them. They lived in isolation from the main stream of evolving life. Relics of an earlier world, somehow still about. They kept on surviving and reproducing from the remote past, through the rise and fall of the dinosaurs, into the age of mammals, still they remained unchanged, still they were capable of finding a living and carrying on their race, no matter how the world changed round them.

'Yet, the curious thing about them is that they are not outdated. They show no signs of atrophy, or senescence, as a species. It now occurs to me that it is not warrantable to assume that they *cannot* evolve further simply because they have not. Could it not be that there was no *need* for them to evolve? After all, their lives impinge so little on other species – except those of the insects, and they easily hold their own against them. No major threat has evolved to challenge them, so why should they evolve? They are almost perfectly adapted to their environment; there is no incentive to evolve. They do very well as they are.

'Now, most species either have to evolve to avoid being superseded, or, if they cannot, they become degenerate. But spiders have not degenerated. Might one not argue from that that they have not *lost* the power to evolve, but that simply because they are so well adapted that there had been no necessity to change, the power remains unused but may still be dormant?'

'I don't know enough about it,' I said. 'It sounds a feasible argument. The chief thing against it that strikes me is any evidence that these spiders have evolved. You yourself told us that they appeared to be perfectly normal.'

'So they do,' she agreed. 'A man also appears to be a perfectly normal mammal – on the dissecting table. It is in his behaviour that he differs from other mammals. It is in their behaviour that these spiders differ from other spiders.'

'You mean hunting in packs?' I asked.

'Exactly. Your normal spider is not a sociable creature. It is an individualist. As such, its first concern is to protect itself from its enemies which it does chiefly by hoping to remain unnoticed. Its second is to feed itself. For this purpose it catches insects, but it does not share them, in fact its disposition is to attack any other spider that approaches, and, if successfully, to eat that as well. Also, in many species the male gets eaten after mating unless he makes a quick get-away. No, a far from sociable creature – and yet, here we have them co-operating. Hunting in packs, as you said. Now, that is so abnormal as to mean a major change of behaviour pattern.'

She broke off, and reflected for a moment.

'That,' she went on, 'is immensely significant – just *how* significant remains to be seen. I should say it's more important than a visible change – like developing better fangs, or even growing wings. It is a sudden manifestation in one species of an attribute which has always been associated with other species – in this case with the ants or the bees. It's the equivalent of finding that a type of monkey, or a breed of dog had suddenly been gifted with the power of reasoning – a characteristic which we have always associated exclusively with the human species.'

'Oh, come,' I objected. 'Isn't that going a bit far?'

'I don't think so. I believe there is a known genus of spiders in which one or two species have learned to live communally, but they are very rare, and insignificant. Nothing on this scale has ever been heard of. If it had, it would certainly be well-known. No, it's a new development – and, to judge from the look of it, a highly successful one . . .'

Before we left we pulled down our veils and sprayed one another with insecticide once more, then we set out on the return journey.

By this time I had gained confidence in our precautions and felt less inclined to run from every band of spiders we encountered among the undergrowth. True, they never failed to swarm to the attack when we approached them, but they seldom climbed further than our knees before they dropped off and scuttled away.

After about a quarter of a mile we found a rocky cleft in the cliffs down which a stream tumbled on its way to the shore below. We turned inland along the side of it in order to find a convenient place for crossing. After a few yards Camilla stopped.

'Just a minute. I want to see this,' she said, and pulled out the glasses. I looked where she pointed.

On the other side of the ravine, on some bushes which crowned a rocky point was a cluster of spiders. They appeared to be doing nothing, just waiting inactively. Then one's eye caught a gleam reflected from a strand of silk which floated in the scarcely moving air. Through the glasses it was possible to see the momentary glistening of several such strands as they wafted in slow, lazy loops.

For some little time nothing apparently happened. Then suddenly a spider ran out from the bush, supported in the empty air. Evidently one of the floating strands had made contact on our side of the ravine, and the spider came across on it speedily and unhesitating. No sooner was he (or she) down on our side than another started on the crossing, then another. After about seven or eight had crossed it the strand of silk became visible. Presently there were three or four spiders making the crossing at the same time, and the single strand had become a definite thread, strong enough now to bear ten or a dozen spiders at once. The rest began to follow, the intervals between them growing shorter, the bridge stronger. We watched until they were all across, perhaps four or five hundred of them, and saw them move off in a clump. Then Camilla lowered her glasses.

'Wonderful stuff, silk,' she said. 'Well, that about puts paid to Charles's plan for an impassable zone, doesn't it?'

We continued on our way thoughtfully.

I made one more discovery just before we got clear of the infested area. A patch of fur caught my eye between stems just to the right of the path we had hacked out. I parted the lower leaves of the bushes, and looked more closely. It was a sizeable rat – at least, it had been; now it was no more than the husk of a rat. Dried, furred skin, empty, and shrivelled over a skeleton that had been picked quite clean . . .

We looked at it for some time without speaking.

# Six

That evening we foregathered with Walter and Charles, and gave an account of our findings. Charles was troubled by our account of the spiders' method of crossing the ravine, but not to the extent of abandoning his plan for a barrier zone.

'Crossing it by that direction would depend on the wind being in the right direction,' he pointed out. 'It's worthwhile as a ground defence. The prevailing wind here appears to be easterly. When there is a change of direction we could keep a special watch.'

Camilla nodded, but doubtfully.

'It depends on numbers,' she said. 'We could probably deal with a few roving bands – particularly if you can contrive some kind of flame-thrower – but if they come in thousands and line up along your perimeter we can't watch every yard of it at once. There aren't enough of us.'

Charles nodded.

'In that case we must clear the ground of bushes and trees well back on the other side of the actual zone,' he suggested. 'If they have no elevation to start from, they can't drift their webs across to make a beginning. But,' he went on, 'your talk of a flame-thrower reminds me. I was thinking today that the best method would be to burn off a belt of land just this side of the infested area to stop them spreading further this way. How effective that would be one can't say, of course, but I imagine it would hold them back for some time, besides killing off great numbers of them. The west wind would be in our favour for that. As a matter of fact, if we got a good enough line of fire going I don't see why it shouldn't spread on and burn off the whole infested side of the island. After all, the first colonists burnt off most of Madeira by accident, and the fires went on for seven years.'

'Madeira,' said Camilla, 'was full of sub-tropical trees. I don't see this place burning like that. Still, it might be worth trying. Even if it did peter out, it ought to clear a zone that would discourage them.'

Eventually it was decided that Camilla and I should go out the following day to prospect a suitable line along which the fires could be started. The idea was, roughly, that we should start out on the path cleared by the exploring party, and then after a mile or so, if the terrain was suitable, or at any rate at some point safely short of that where the exploring party had encountered the spiders, we should turn off to the left and start cutting a new path roughly parallel to the coastline, and later extend it to the right.

'I'm sorry I can't let you have help yet,' Charles told us. 'But the number one priority just now is getting the mess-hall building up and finished. When everybody knows that there is a safe retreat available in case of need it will calm them down a lot. Half of them are afraid to go to sleep at present for fear of waking up to discover they've been overrun by spiders. But once that is done we shall be able to relax a little and spare some of them. In any case, this seems to be a settled calm spell, and it wouldn't be any good starting fires until we have a wind – and the right kind of wind – to get them to take hold. But if you'll start to cut the tracks it will mark out the line, ready for when the time comes.'

There was a slight smile at the corners of Camilla's mouth.

'What Charles really means,' she explained, 'is that everyone is anxious to go no nearer spider territory than he can possibly help.' She shook her head. 'Men like gods – well, well,' she muttered. Then she turned to me. 'What about you, Arnold?'

'I don't mind admitting that it wouldn't have taken much to make me cry off this morning. But as far as getting to know our enemy is concerned this has been an educational day. Yes, I'll come,' I told her.

Early the following morning we set off, equipped as we had been on the previous day. Two hundred yards or so along the beach we turned off on to the track that the exploring party had followed. It was rough going. The party had cleared enough width to allow them a passage, but no more. We were closed in by bushes and trees that were nameless to me, so that visibility was never more than a foot or two to either side, and little more ahead. No place for anyone with a tendency to claustrophobia. Occasionally there were thickets of strong, tall grasses which showed me for the first time the literal meaning of the word bamboozled. The short range of vision made it difficult to judge distance. We just seemed to go on and on until we had a feeling that we must be traversing the same ground again and again. It all seemed to be flat, too, although one knew that the ground must be gradually rising. After three-quarters of an hour of it, I paused. We still had not encountered any signs of spiders.

'How much further?' I asked.

'I should say we're over halfway,' Camilla judged.

'Oh,' I said. We went on.

After another half-hour I began to see occasional strands of web among the bushes beside us. I was about to draw Camilla's attention to them when the matter settled itself. She was in the lead then, and her shoulder brushed a frond as she passed. Immediately, a stream of spiders rushed from it on to her. Simultaneously, a clump of them dropped from the branch above. For a moment her head and shoulders were almost obscured under them. Then they hurriedly began to drop off. They did not like the insecticide any more than the others had. In a few moments they were all on the ground, scurrying away.

Camilla stopped and looked around. The foliage was too dense to show whether there were other bands lurking in it.

'We've found their frontier. I'd rather not go further,' she said.

At the thought of what must lie in the undergrowth not far ahead, I agreed.

We decided to go back along the track for twenty minutes, and then, if that brought us to a spot where the way looked passable, to make a start on our fire line in a northerly direction. That, we thought, should give a wide enough strip of country to make it pretty certain there were no spiders behind us.

As luck would have it the twenty minutes did bring us to a likely place where the bushes, though thorned, were light and easy to clear with our machetes.

'This'll do,' Camilla said sitting down on a fallen tree-trunk.

'We can make a start here,' I said, cautiously. 'By the look of it we're bound to meet thickets whichever way we go. It'll be slow work.'

She pulled out a packet of cigarettes and offered me one. I took it and sat down on the trunk beside her.

'From your tone I gather you don't think much of Charles's plan?' she said.

'Oh, I think it's a good idea,' I told her. 'But I hadn't seen all this then.' I waved my hand at the surrounding growth. 'Two of us aren't going to make much impression on it, are we?'

'We can try. It hasn't got to be a straight line. We can stick to the easier patches as long as we keep the general direction right.'

We sat and smoked in silence for some moments. Presently she said: 'I was thinking about this spider thing last night. It could be much bigger than we imagine, you know. Something has happened to these spiders, something inside them. Outwardly they are just normal spiders, but they are spiders *plus* something other spiders don't have . . .'

'That's practically what you said after you'd examined the first one,' I pointed out.

'Yes, I know, but I hadn't thought out the possible implications then. The thing that suddenly struck me last night is their power of adaptation, of employing the resources they have.

'One supposes that the original purpose of spider silk was simply to make a cocoon to keep the eggs safe. But then, when the insects learnt to fly, the spiders found a new use for the silk. They began to weave webs to catch the flying insects. Having discovered one use of their silk they went on to employ it in all sorts of ways – and to make specialized silks. They built nests of it, with trapdoors to close them, they spun sheet webs into which passing insects fell, and the more advanced types evolved the orb web. They used it for tying up their prey, for stitching leaves together to make a home, they bound leaves to their webs to hide them as they waited. They even used it for building bridges, and for flying with – as we saw yesterday.

'Well, bearing in mind what they could do with the power to make silk, I began to wonder what they could do with this new power, to co-operate. It's quite frightening, really. It has already brought them into conflict with species which were right outside their orbit, and apparently with such success that they have practically cleared this island of most other forms of animate life. It has even brought them into conflict with us – and the first blood went to them. I got to wondering whether we aren't seeing the beginning of a revolution; the beginning of a takeover of power . . .'

'That,' I said, with restraint, 'was surely rather a small-hours nightmare. A takeover of a small isolated island where everything is in their favour is one thing. On the mainland they could be efficiently tackled.'

'How would you do that? You can't burn off *all* the forests in the world. A species continues to exist by outbreeding the checks that its natural enemies impose on it. That is what gives the illusion of "the balance of nature" belief. Once the natural enemies cease to be a threat its fecundity becomes terrifying. Look what has happened in a generation or two to our own population, largely because a few diseases have been overcome. Find a way of conquering the natural enemies, and the only limiting factor is the food supply. Well, these spiders have found a way, and clearly their fecundity is formidable. The need for food and their ability to tackle new sources of food is driving them on. As long as they can find food and so continue to breed it is difficult to see what can stop them.'

'But it's fantastic to consider them as a serious threat,' I protested, 'I'll accept your thesis that something has happened inside them which has changed their habits – made them social instead of individual – and that conditions here were favourable for them. But that isn't enough to turn them into a major threat.'

'I don't know. Becoming social may have implications we haven't seen yet. It has had immense implications with the ants and the bees. They are now the original spiders plus something, as I said. It remains to be discovered just what that plus is.'

'I still don't see –'

'No? Let me tell you a Cinderella story,' said Camilla. 'Once upon a time there was a timid lemur-like creature that lurked in the forests, just as a lot of the other animals did. It wasn't strong, it had no claws, quite unformidable teeth. It survived by keeping out of trouble. But in the course of time something happened to it that changed it. It remained still a mammal, but it was *plus* something indefinable inside it . . . And because of that mysterious plus it rose to be Lord of the animal creation, Master of the World . . .

'Because that happened once, it can happen again. There is rise, and there is fall. None of us is here forever. If that could happen to that little lemur-creature, it could happen to any creature.'

'But not, for heaven's sake, not to *spiders* . . .!'

'And *why* not to spiders?' demanded Camilla. 'Mind is only a phenomenon which distinguishes the present dominant species. The rest of creation gets along all right without it. But there are powers other than mind. Again I refer you to the termites and the bees, they build complicated structures and run complex societies without the use of mind, they co-operate for defence and attack without a directing mind. Mind, for all we know, is just a flash in the pan, interesting as a phenomenon, but unnecessary. Dominate today, gone tomorrow . . .'

'And then back to a world dominated by instincts?' I asked.

'Instinct – is such a treacherous word. It only means something "touched in" – by God's finger? It is a confession of failure to understand why a thing happens – a mere admission that it does happen that way. It explains nothing.

'It is just too easy to say that a bee builds a perfectly hexagonal cell by "instinct", or that a spider constructs a mathematically sound orb web by "instinct" – *and* it flies in the face of all we know about the transmission of acquired characteristics.

'No, there is something else. And there is corporate sensitivity, too – the fact that the ant army *knows* when to defend or attack, that the worker bee *knows* its work and its place in the hive, even that a flock of birds *knows* when to wheel or dive as one. It is not mind at work – but it *is* transmission of some kind . . .

'Now, do you see what I'm getting at? Obviously these spiders have acquired this power of transmission – that is their *plus*. What remains to be discovered is the degree to which they have it. It could well be in excess of the degree normal in other species . . . Those we saw yesterday when we were sitting on the headland looked remarkably efficiently organized.'

I crushed out the end of my cigarette.

'Look,' I said, 'we came here to do a job, not to weave horrid fantasies. Isn't it time we got on with it?'

'All right,' she agreed, unsheathing her machete.

I consulted the compass, and we went to work.

The path we cut was tortuous, but labour-saving. When we found ourselves faced by a dense thicket we went round it, or at least found a place where it was not so dense, and cut through there. We deviated similarly for clumps of trees and intimidating thorn-bushes, but we averaged the right direction. Progress was, however, slow and the making of it wearisome. Nor was it helped by Camilla's tendency to forget work when something professionally interesting caught her attention. After an hour of hacking had taken us perhaps a hundred and fifty yards, we felt it was time for some refreshment, and cleared a space where we could sit in moderate comfort.

This time Camilla was not inclined to air her theories. She sat, evolving new ones, I suspected, while she munched her sandwiches with a contemplative air. As we sat I became aware of the intensity of the silence that surrounded us. Normally, in such a place one would be surrounded by sounds: the cries of birds, the rustle, scamperings, or slitherings of unseen small creatures, the constant hum of insects, a murmurous background pierced now and then by harsh calls, but here there was nothing more than the occasional drone of a rare winged insect, and the sound of our munching, to break it. After a time it began to get on my nerves. More to break it than for interest I said:

'This kind of thing must have a natural term. When they've wiped out every living thing here they must just come to an end, and die off.'

'Spiders are cannibals,' said Camilla.

'Even so – well, I mean a closed cannibal economy scarcely seems practicable.'

'Perhaps not, but it would work for a time – until, as I said, they learn to catch fish. Then the food supply will cease to be a problem, and there'll be nothing to stop them.'

'But how on earth can they catch fish?'

She shrugged.

'Co-operation makes many things possible. Working together they could weave a strong net. I imagine they'll start by laying it across a narrow inlet, anchored by stones. When the tide is up they could raise it, and wait for the tide to go down. It would trap shrimps and small fish. Success would make them more ambitious. They'll go after bigger fish, and invent new methods of catching them.'

'You're talking of them as if they were reasoning creatures.'

'That's what troubles me. Clearly they cannot reason as we understand it – by a process of brain and mind. But there must, as I said before, be something akin to reason at work. Something that inspired them first with the idea of using the web to catch insects, and then went on to inspire them farther to build the complex, carefully designed webs that the higher forms do. Plenty of insects can produce kinds of silk. But only the spiders learnt to develop it in order to use it as a weapon and a means of livelihood. It wasn't by the kind of intelligence we know, but there was a guiding force of some kind – there *must* have been.

'And that took place among individualists. Now we have them acting socially. Co-operation introduces a factor which is greater than the sum of its parts. What could a man become, alone?

'So, if this force guided individualists to develop a means of catching flying insects, it can certainly guide a co-operative group of them to develop a means of catching fish when the need arises. What's troubling me is how far does this thing go – what else may it guide them to develop . . .?'

'Frankly,' I told her, 'I think you're magnifying the whole thing. What we have here is a freak development given, by pure chance, ideal conditions for survival and breeding. It will breed to the limit of its food supply, and then just peter out. It must have happened hundreds of times in the world's history that a species has killed itself off by its own fecundity.'

'I hope you're right . . .' she said, without conviction.

We resumed our hacking. For another twenty yards we made the same slow progress as before. Then with utter unexpectedness we emerged upon a track, and stopped, staring.

The track ran east and west, at right angles to our own. Furthermore, it was a track that had been well, and recently, used. We stood there looking right and left to where turns in it cut off our view.

'Robinson Crusoe and the footprint,' murmured Camilla. 'Didn't one of the children say something about –?'

She broke off suddenly as the bushes facing us parted to reveal two dark faces, and two spears levelled at us.

For a moment we simply stared. Then I took a firmer grip of my machete. The spear that was trained on me quivered.

'Drop it,' said a voice.

I hesitated, and watched the spear quiver again.

I dropped it.

Camilla dropped hers, too.

There was a rustling behind us. Dark, shining arms reached forward and picked up the machetes. Hands patted us gently. One of them found Charles's revolver in Camilla's pocket, and removed it. The spears in front, though still levelled at us, became less tense. Their owners stepped out on to the track.

Both men were naked except for a loin-cloth and moccasin-like shoes, but they wore belts to support machetes in scabbards and a kind of harness which carried two or three more short spears. The most noticeable thing about them was the way their dark skins gleamed. From their shoes to the top of their fuzzy hair they shone as if they had been french-polished all over. Whatever they had used to anoint themselves gave off a sharp, powerful, though not altogether unpleasant odour.

One of them, without lowering his spear, held out his left hand. A shining brown arm reached forward from behind us and put the revolver in it. The man stepped back, stuck his spear into the harness, and examined the revolver with satisfaction. Having assured himself that all the chambers were loaded, he slipped off the safety-catch, pointed it at me, and motioned to my right.

There was no arguing with that. We turned, and set off along the path in the easterly direction.

Round the first bend a voice behind us ordered: 'Stop', and we stopped. Close beside as at the side of the track lay four bags, each the size of a small sack. They looked to me to be made of a fabric formed of closely woven strips of palm-leaf.

We waited while some kind of discussion went on behind us. I received a nudge from Camilla's right elbow, and looked round to see her attention fixed on one of the bags. For a moment I wondered why; then I noticed that the bag was not quite inert. It seemed to be undulating slightly. Presently I was quite sure that there was a kind of seething movement going on inside it. I glanced at the other bags; they, too, showed signs of a slow stirring within.

'What –?' I was beginning in a whisper, when the discussion behind us came to an end.

Our arms were seized and brought behind, and our wrists securely, though not painfully, tied together.

'Go on,' ordered the voice.

I glanced back as we left.

One man was following a short distance behind us, revolver in hand. Beyond him the other three were raising bags on to their backs; the fourth bag remained where it lay.

I reckoned that the meeting with the Islanders must have been a piece of sheer bad luck for us. They, on their way along the track, would have heard the sounds of our hacking and crashing progress, and dumped their loads in order to investigate. Having contrived their simple ambush, and left one of their number to look after us, the rest had continued on their interrupted journey westwards. The most disquieting feature was that we were now being herded in the opposite direction, straight into spider country.

After a quarter of a mile or so we encountered our first band of them. It must have been lurking close beside the track for it emerged from cover a few yards ahead, making briskly towards us.

'Stop!' commanded the voice behind us.

We obeyed. The spiders came on charging at our feet and starting to climb our legs. As before, they reached knee-level and dropped off. The man behind us was evidently observing the encounter, for I heard him give a grunt. Then he said: 'Go on.'

Camilla, however, turned round.

'My veil,' she said, nodding her head in an attempt to dislodge it from where it was rolled up on her hat brim.

The man stared uncomprehendingly for a moment, then he got the idea. He stepped forward, the pistol still in his right hand, and with his left hand freed the veil so that it fell in front of her face. As he did so I noticed that the spiders made no attempt to attack him. At a distance of four or five inches from his feet they stopped and sheered off. It was evident that the oil with which he was smeared was a more potent deterrent than our insecticide.

He turned to me, and twitched my veil so that the front of it fell loosely down, too. Then we went on.

Before long another band of spiders came scuttling to the attack, then another. Presently we were encountering them every few yards. Twice they dropped on us from overhanging bushes. Without the protection of the veils we should have had them swarming on our faces; even with the veils there were a few unpleasant moments before they let go and dropped off.

As we went on I realized that the track we were following was, like the track we had followed from the beach, an old path recently cleared. I could not use my compass to check the direction, but I judged it to run roughly a few degrees further to the north than the other. It had obviously been wider, too, and more used, which, in spite of the overgrowth, had made it easier to clear a passage.

Soon I began to notice strands of web among the bushes on either side. At first they were haphazard threads, but quite quickly we reached a part where they were woven into small sheets like irregularly shaped hammocks slung between the branches of a bush, or between one bush and the next. These hammocks occurred in clusters, each cluster apparently the communal property of a group of spiders who waited around them ready to pounce upon anything that fell into them. It seemed a poor prospect in a region almost entirely denuded of insects, and I did not see a single instance of anything trapped in them. The spiders seemed prepared to wait patiently, indefinitely.

When we passed close enough to them for them to see us, or in some other way to be aware of our movements, they ceased all of a sudden to be inactive, and came swarming out along branches or on the ground to intercept us. Usually they were too late. We had passed before they reached a strategic point for attack, but occasionally the leaders arrived in time to drop down on us, or to reach our feet.

As we went on the hammocks of web at our level grew infrequent. They gave way to heavier hammocks slung between branches ten or twelve feet from the ground which made the chances of anything falling into lower webs slender indeed.

Presently we entered a zone where even the larger web hammocks no longer stretched between trees. They hung in tatters from the branches, stirring slightly in the moving air. The whole forest seemed to drip with gently undulating rags of silk.

Camilla who was in the lead, stopped, and looked around.

'Ghostly,' she said. 'Hung with graveclothes.'

Her voice sounded loud in the silence of the place.

It occurred to me that some of the ghostly effect was due to the poor light, and looked upwards. I couldn't see the sky. The tree tops disappeared into a translucent whitish fog, and I realized that we must now be under the white pall we had seen in the distance.

It was as if the whole forest had been tented over. The web was spread in a continuous sheet from treetop to treetop, and the spiders were up there with it. There were none on the ground now, nor did I recollect seeing any for some little time.

All around us was the eerie silence of an utterly deserted place. Every creature, including the spiders themselves, had left it, only the plants, the bushes, and the trees lived on. Nothing moved save for the abandoned hanks of web with ragged fringes slowly swirling.

'Go on,' ordered the voice behind us.

The ground began to rise now, but for half a mile the scene round us remained the same.

Only once did I see anything move. Then it was a patch of shadow, crawling across our path. I looked up and saw a dark patch sliding slowly over the white tegument, a band of spiders prowling its airy territory.

The trees came to an end quite suddenly. We emerged from them on to open hillside covered with some close, knee-high, heather-like growth. On the fringe of it we encountered hunting bands of spiders again and the first few feet of it was thick with their webs, but beyond that they quickly grew fewer. Whether it was something in the nature of the ground, or some quality in the heather-like plants, or the altitude, or the poverty of the pickings that deterred them, one could not say, but whatever the reason we presently found ourselves free of them.

We went on climbing steadily up the flank of Monu, the more southern of the twin hills, until we reached the lip of the crater at the top. There our captor allowed us to sit down for a few minutes rest.

The situation gave us the best view of Tanakuatua we had yet had – and a very curious sight it was. The whole of the east coast round to where the northern summit cut off our view was spread with the slightly greyed sheet of web, and it continued to the south, with an arm of it reaching northward between the hill and the lagoon. It was as if it had come from the east and had flowed round the hill and now the northward arm had already covered nearly half the distance between the hill and the settlement. There it ended. The strip of clear country which separated it from the settlement was something like a mile and a half wide, and the whole west coast north of that was clear of it, too. How far it stretched inland from the northern part of the east coast, the other hill made it impossible for us to see, but it was clear that fully half of the whole island lay under it.

It lay as if it had been held taut and allowed to fall over the uneven surface, humped in places by the taller trees beneath, gleaming where the folds caught the light. Round the edge it was not completely continuous. In places there were detached patches looking like rags torn off the main body and carelessly dropped, and, as if to show that water was no barrier, small patches of it were visible on the islet of Hinuati.

Our captor, sitting beside us, caught our expressions as we gazed at it. He grinned, but said nothing.

In two or three places, as on the previous days, there were faint columns like attenuated steam rising skyward.

Camilla shook her head.

'Astronomical numbers. The mind boggles,' she said.

We turned our attention to the crater below us. It was rather wider and shallower than I had expected, surprising, too, to find grass and weeds and small bushes growing more than halfway down its inside slope. Beyond them was a zone of bare rock, and then, in the middle of the saucer, a pool of hot mud bubbling sluggishly.

I supposed that it was boiling, but it was the most leisurely boil I had ever seen. It seethed with a lazy, slow-motion quality as though making a reluctant effort. Every now and then it started to blow a larger bubble. While this was going on the rest seemed to subside somewhat, as though all the energy available were going into the bubble blowing. The dome-like bubble was disturbing. It was impossible to watch the thing grow without building up a sympathetic tension, waiting for the burst. And the burst, when it came, was an anti-climax: just a dull, tired plop, and a scatter of mud for a few feet around. After that it seethed gently for a while, blowing a few smaller bubbles for practice before starting on another big one.

'Curious,' said Camilla. 'Like a lot of other natural processes it's a bit disgusting, but I can suddenly see quite clearly how a thing like that can become sacred. To a simple mind it could easily seem to be alive – or sort of alive, in a different way from other things. It just lies there – and by the look of it it's lain there for centuries – doing nothing but go glug-glug, yet somehow there's an ominous feeling that it might do more at any moment. It's not surprising people get the urge to propitiate them.'

We sat there for a bit longer watching the mud bubbles bloat like horrid stomachs filling, waiting in fascinated distaste for the soggy plops of their collapse. Our captor, too, seemed unable to take his eyes off them. After a time, however, he rose, and motioned us on to our feet again with the pistol.

We went on round the rim of the crater until we came to the saddle joining it to the other hill. There we turned left and kept to the top of the ridge. It was easy walking on coarse, wiry grass. Halfway along it was an arrangement of stones, forming a kind of rectangular table about three feet high, set at a slight, obviously intentional, angle to the run of the ridge. We looked at it curiously. It was the sole constructional work of the former inhabitants that we had seen since we landed: possibly their only monument. It had been carefully built, too, and topped with a couple of flat stones.

'Could it be some sort of altar?' Camilla suggested.

When we reached it any doubt about that was dispelled. The top of it was smeared with dark, caked blood.

We had no time to stop and examine it. Our guard marched us on past it.

An unpleasant possibility began to trouble me. I hesitated, then I said:

'Do you think –?'

Camilla cut me short. The same idea had evidently occurred to her. 'No,' she said. 'It's been there for a week at least, probably longer. Besides, there wasn't enough of it.' After a pause, she added: 'All the same, it'd be interesting to know what they found here to make a sacrifice.'

The ridge came to an end. There were some two hundred yards of hillside to climb. Then we found ourselves on the rim of the northern crater.

This one had clearly been inactive for a very long time. Slips of rock from the sides had blocked it long enough ago for soil to form. Clumps of vegetation clung to the walls, and down at the bottom were thickets of bushes and a sizeable grove of trees. A rough path led zig-zag down the crater wall towards them.

Our guard startled both of us by giving a loud hail, which echoed back and forth across the crater.

Presently two dark-skinned men emerged from the trees and stood at the foot of the path, looking up.

Our captor shouted something unintelligible, and received an equally unintelligible reply. He slipped the revolver into his belt and drew his machete. With it he cut the cords on our wrists before urging us down the path ahead of him.

It was as well he did. The way was steep, and tricky in places. I doubt whether I could have made it with my arms tied together.

At the bottom we walked towards the two men who stood waiting for us.

One of them I recognized at once. He had been noticeably older than the rest of the party we had taken aboard at Uijanji. It was the streaks of grey in his fuzzy black hair that identified him for me. Without that I should not have known him as he was now, clad only in a loin cloth like the others, and with a bone ornament piercing the septum of his nostrils.

But he was ornamented in another way, too. A design had been daubed on his chest with yellow paint like a crude heraldic emblem. The centre of the device was a pearshaped blob. From it radiated eight strokes, each hooked at the end. The significance of it was lost on me until I noticed Camilla stare at it fixedly, and raise her eyes to the man's face with a puzzled look in them. Then I looked at the emblem again and suddenly saw it for what it was: a childlike representation of a spider . . .

# Seven

The man with the spider emblem looked at us briefly, and then turned to question our captor. He listened thoughtfully to the reply and put several more questions. Then he turned to his companion, and gave an order. The man stepped forward and laid hold of my haversack. It would have been pointless to resist. I let go.

They discovered the spray-gun, sniffed at it, nodded, unscrewed the filler cap and poured the contents on to the ground. Then they discovered the spare tin of insecticide and that, too, was poured away. The rest of the contents did not interest them. They took Camilla's haversack, dealt similarly with her spray-gun, and threw it away.

The ornamented man regarded us again. He stepped closer, lifted my arm, sniffed at my sleeve, and nodded.

'Take off your clothes,' he said, in English. 'You too,' he added, to Camilla.

When we hesitated our captor made a move with his machete. There was nothing for it but to obey. I was allowed to retain my pants, and Camilla her panties. Both of us kept our shoes.

The third man bundled our discarded clothing together and carried it off into the trees. The ornamented man turned to our captor and said something, holding out his hand. With some reluctance the other drew the revolver from his belt, and passed it to him, then at a gesture of dismissal turned and started back up the wall of the crater. The ornamented man examined the revolver with satisfaction before thrusting it into his own belt. He turned to regard us for a moment, then, without speaking, made his way back into the trees, leaving us alone. We watched him until he disappeared.

Camilla sat down on the ground.

'And that's that,' she said. 'Very simple. Very effective.'

It required no comment from me. There was no need to guard us. Without our clothing to protect us from the spiders we could not attempt to go back by the way we had come. Without machetes to clear a path we could not hope to make our way north and then west keeping clear of spider country – nor could we be sure that we were indeed keeping clear of it. It was, as she said, very simple.

I dropped down beside her, and we sat for some little time in silent contemplation of the situation.

Presently Camilla shook her head.

'I don't understand it,' she said. 'They could easily have killed us. The others would simply have thought the spiders had got us. Why didn't they?'

'Come to that, why did they want to jump the ship and stay here, at all?' I countered.

There was silence for some moments.

'Why,' she asked uneasily, 'should they carry spiders about in those bags?'

'*If* it was spiders in them,' I said.

'Of course it was. The contents were moving, weren't they? What else could it have been?' she replied impatiently.

We pondered that, too, for a time.

I gave it up, and reached for my haversack, still lying where it had been dropped. The contents, save for the spray and the insecticide, were intact: even the field-glasses which I should have expected to arouse covctousness – except, of course, that they were of little use hemmed in as we were by the crater wall. There was also the remains of our food. I gave Camilla a sandwich, and took one myself.

After that we shared a bar of chocolate. Then there was nothing to do.

The sun sank lower. The shadow of the crater wall crept over us. We decided to move into the trees and collect branches and leaves to give us a couch and at least a sort of covering for the night. What we achieved was far from comfortable. In spite of the layer of leaves the branches formed hard ridges, twigs scratched and dug into sensitive parts, furthermore as there were no spiders here there were insects. Also our attempts to cover ourselves with leaves, at least, to keep ourselves covered with leaves, were unsuccessful.

Soon after darkness had fallen the two Islanders lit a fire. We lay and watched its flickering through the trees for an hour or more. Camilla moved restlessly. Suddenly she sat up.

'Damn this,' she said, decisively. 'Come what may, I'm going to get warm by that fire.'

'You can't do that,' I protested. 'You'll probably be – well, I mean to say, it'd be asking for trouble.'

She got to her feet.

'I don't care,' she announced. 'It couldn't be more uncomfortable than this.' And she started to walk off.

I perforce followed her.

The two Islanders were sitting close to the fire staring into the flames. They couldn't have helped hearing our approach, but we might not have existed for all the notice they took of us. Camilla kept straight on. Even when we were quite close they neither turned their heads, nor seemed to see us. We walked to the other side of the fire. There Camilla, with an appearance of confidence that I was far from feeling, sat down and held out her hands to the blaze. I followed suit, hoping that I looked as calm as she did. Still neither of the men moved.

After some minutes the second man leaned forward. With a twig he stirred something that was cooking in a cut-down tin can. As he leant back again, I became aware that the ornamented man, without moving, was watching us.

I tried to judge his expression, but the uncertain light, as well as the effect on his countenance of his bone spike through his nose, made it difficult to determine. His eyes, gleaming now and then as they caught the flames were steady. I decided that they looked more contemplative than dangerous.

After a period of prolonged and reflective study he asked, without any preliminary:

'Why you come here?'

Camilla stretched her hands to the fire again.

'To keep warm,' she said.

Without any change of expression the man said:

'Why you come to Tanakuatua?'

Camilla looked at him thoughtfully.

'Why are you here? Isn't Tanakuatua tabu for you? It is not tabu for us.'

The man frowned.

'Tanakuatua is tabu for all men – and women, too. We came only to help the Little Sisters. It is permitted.' He frowned again, and went on: 'Tanakuatua is our island, our home, ours.'

Camilla said, mildly:

'We were given to understand that it was sold to the British Government, who sold it to us.'

'Tanakuatua was taken from us by a trick,' the man started.

Camilla looked interested.

'What was this trick?' she asked.

The man did not reply at once. He regarded us both as if making up his mind. Then he decided to tell the story.

'It was in the time of Nokiki, my father . . .' he began. He told us the tale in fluent English, his occasionally quaint phrases and unfamiliar turns of speech giving it an added fascination, so there by the fire which the other man fed with an occasional handful of sticks, we heard for the first time of the Curse of Nokiki, and his sacrifice. The account was, not unnaturally, somewhat biased, but the man, whose name we now learned to be Naeta, gave it with sincerity and emotion. Those parts of it we were able to check later differed from it only in unimportant details – and in the point of view.

The tale took some time in telling, but once started Naeta was not to be diverted. Twice in the course of it the other man offered him the food cooking in the tin, but each time he waved it aside, and the other man with a shrug returned it to the embers to keep warm. Not until he had finished, leaving us with a picture of the last four Tanakuatuans paddling their canoe away across the empty ocean, leaving their forbidden island behind them for ever, did he take up the tin and help himself to its contents.

We sat silent until he had finished, then Camilla said:

'But, surely, if you could not live here again, the only sensible thing to do was to sell the island?'

Naeta glared at her grimly.

'We did not sell, Tanakuatua is ours,' he said angrily.

He went on to explain that there had been compensation paid.

It was only right that the Government who had tricked them into leaving the island, and so was responsible for the curse that was put on it, should find them another place to live, but that did not mean that they had *sold* their island. Neither they nor anyone else could live there, so why should they sell it, and why should anyone be willing to buy it? It was useless, therefore it stood to reason that no one had bought it. But though it was no longer of use, it remained their island. They had conquered it, they had held it, and it was there that the bones of their ancestors rested. They had accepted the situation – until they had heard that the Government had tricked them again by selling Tanakuatua, which was not theirs to sell.

At this point he became so heated, and his account so involved that we could not follow it then. Only by patient inquiries later did I manage to get it more or less sorted out.

Apparently the news that Tanakuatua had been sold reached the Tanakuatuan exiles in their new home on the island of Imu as a rumour, but even unconfirmed it had immediately aroused strong feelings. When it was later authenticated it split the community into several factions.

Kusake, now Chief in succession to his father, Tatake, was shocked, but he was not a man to be governed by his reflexes. From his father he had learnt, both by precept and example, the qualities required of a contemporary Chief. He fully understood, as some of his people still did not, that whatever the provocations of injustice, the modern world held a very poor future for a romantic leader of warriors. Legendary heroes were a part of a proud history, still to be venerated, but no longer to be imitated. The task of a Chief, in the ebb of his people's fortunes, was to hold them together, to prevent the tribe from disintegrating, to conserve its entity against the time when the tide should turn again. Until that happened the leader must be primarily politician; and warriors, workers. Valour must be hidden beneath cunning; ferocity beneath cold determination. Pride and faith must be kept burning – but in a darkened lantern.

Kusake's private views regarding the sale of Tanakuatua were emotionally confused, but as a politician he saw the situation clearly: the British Government had not only deprived them of their homeland, it had then gone on to sell that homeland for a sum far in excess of that paid in compensation, thus making a handsome profit on the deal; the Government had been guilty of sharp practice in selling an island under a tabu to a purchaser who would not be able to make use of it. The whole affair was nothing less than a crying scandal from several points of view. Having considered the matter, Kusake decided upon plans A and B. Plan A was to take legal advice. Should that be discouraging, plan B was to appeal to those members of the Opposition who had been responsible for contriving the move from the reservation to Imu, to raise the matter in the House.

Unfortunately, however sound this approach may have been in policy, it lacked appeal to the more vigorous of his subjects, and opposition to it crystallized around Naeta.

Naeta, son of Nokiki, had as a young man been one of the three who had kept his father company on Tanakuatua until the last. This had brought him considerable prestige, and led, in the course of time, to his succeeding his father as chief medicine man of the tribe.

His indignation over the sale of the island went even further than his Chief's in claiming that Tanakuatua was not even the property of the Government to sell. The compensation, he asserted, was not money given in purchase; it was a conscience-payment, since it was as a result of the Government's action that Tanakuatua now lay under tabu.

Furthermore, Nokiki's stand and eventual self-sacrifice had made the island, though forbidden, forever sacred ground to the tribe, and doubly sacred to members of Nokiki's totem-clan.

In such circumstances the claim which Kusake was proposing, and which, if successful, would result in merely another monetary gesture of compensation, was nugatory and irrelevant. He was indeed shocked that the honour and sacred places of a proud people should be considered matters for barter. It was a disgrace to set the ghosts of their ancestors wailing in the Happy Land. The time had come for action.

Dancer-on-the-Waves, who also held prestige as the woman who had been privileged to weave Nokiki's burial mat, took a variant of this view. It was known, she said, that a dreadful form of death now awaited all who set foot on Tanakuatua. Nakaa had kept faith with Nokiki. Therefore there was no need to take action as Naeta was suggesting. What was important now, she insisted, was for them to show their faith in Nakaa; to do homage to him, to make repentance for their sins, to atone for the weakness of those who had strayed towards the white God, to confess the lack of faith which had rendered them incapable of defending their own island, thus bringing Nokiki's curse upon it; and to pray for just vengeance to fall upon their enemies.

To this Naeta retorted that to leave all the work of retribution to Nakaa would be evidence that they were still a spiritless people. If they were to continue to let matters drift while strangers dwelt on the sacred ground and trampled the groves of their ancestors, no one need be surprised when new, and worse, tribulations fell upon them. What was needed now was positive affirmation of faith in Nakaa's laws; deeds of dedication; action, not on their own behalf, but on Nakaa's: action which would restore them to the favour of the old gods, and set the ghosts of their ancestors rejoicing.

The old and the middle-aged divided, some in favour of Kusake's policy, some supporting Dancer-on-the-Waves. The young too, were divided, but differently. Some of the men who, as Tatake had complained, had ceased to believe in anything, remained cynical, though interested in any further compensation that might be extracted; but there were others who rallied to Naeta, and held councils of action.

One of the stumbling blocks was finance. Several plans were laid before Kusake and the elders. Each as forthrightly rejected until it became quite clear that any hope of assistance from the tribal treasury was in vain.

'Very well,' proclaimed Naeta, 'these timid men have shown us where we stand. Our valiant ancestors had no need of this white man's invention of money. Their wealth was the goodwill of the gods. So let us do what they would have done. Let us pray to the gods for guidance. If we show faith in them, they will show us how we may become instruments of their vengeance.'

For many months the gods had appeared to be deaf. Then, one day, came the news that an agent in Uijanji was attempting to enlist a party to help with the landing on Tanakuatua. Unsurprisingly, in view of the island's well-known reputation, he was having no success.

When he heard this Naeta became thoughtful, and after a time he thanked the gods for showing him the way.

In the evening he called his followers together, and outlined his plan.

Naeta's account as he talked to us beside the fire was confusing, and we made little of it. One thing, however, was clear, and it puzzled Camilla.

'You have deliberately come to an island that is tabu. I don't understand that.'

He nodded seriously.

'Nakaa understands,' he told her. 'He knows that we come only to do his work. To help the Little Sisters. We do not come to live here. So he permits it, and we are safe.'

'I see – a dispensation,' murmured Camilla. 'There is always a way of getting round a rule . . .'

Naeta disregarded that. He looked at her intently, and repeated his original question:

'Now you tell me why you came here.'

'All right,' agreed Camilla, and she gave him an outline of the Project.

How much he understood of it was impossible to tell. He listened motionless and expressionless, his eyes fixed unwaveringly on the flames. I, for my part, heard her with a sense of utter detachment. The scheme which had sounded so feasible back home, with all the resources which Lord Foxfield's money could buy to back it, had become increasingly unreal ever since we landed. Now it was as irrelevant and insubstantial as a pipe-dream.

She ended by explaining that Tanakuatua had been chosen as a place where the community could develop a life of its own, free from outside interference.

He looked up as she finished, and shook his head slowly.

'There is no place in the world like that. No more,' he said.

'You could be right,' Camilla agreed, 'but it seemed possible. This small island, lost in a great ocean . . .'

'You know about the tabu, but you did not care. White men laugh at tabu, I know. It is foolish, very foolish. You did not know about the Little Sisters.'

'You keep on talking about the Little Sisters. Who are they?'

For an answer Naeta touched his finger to the sign on his chest.

'Oh, the spiders. No, we did not know about them. Why do you call them the Little Sisters?'

'Because they are *my* Little Sisters. Nakaa caused them to spring from the corruption of my father, Nokiki's body. Therefore they are sisters, and brothers, to me.'

He paused. Camilla forebore to comment. He went on:

'They are the messengers of Nakaa. He has sent them to punish the world. As he once turned men and women out of the Happy Land, now he is going to turn them out of the world. It is his vengeance: the Little Sisters are his instrument. Now they are only in Tanakuatua, but he has taught them how to fly. Already they are setting out on winds which will take them to all the corners of the earth.'

Camilla nodded.

'Yes, we have seen that.'

'Where they land, they will breed; and when they breed enough they will carry the tabu that is on Tanakuatua over the whole world. That will be the vengeance of Nakaa.'

Camilla pondered, and then shook her head.

'I don't think I understand – vengeance for what?'

'For lack of faith,' Naeta told her. 'In the old days,' he explained, 'the people obeyed the commands of Nakaa the judge, the lawgiver. They honoured their totems, they preserved their shrines, they revered the bones of their ancestors, they performed the burial rites according to his laws in order that when their ghosts came before him for judgement he might not strangle them, or throw them on the stakes in the Pits, but would open the door to the Paradise of the Shades where they would live in happiness forever.

'For many, many generations upright men and their sons obeyed these laws, and, through their faith, their ghosts went to dwell in Paradise – the others went into the pits.

'But then the white men came. They brought evil weapons, evil diseases, the evil of money, the evil of greed. But, worst of all, they destroyed faith by showing that these evils were stronger than the virtues. They respected neither the laws of Nakaa, nor the customs of men and women – yet no disaster struck them. With all their evils they remained powerful.

'Many of our people, seeing this began to doubt. They lost faith in Nakaa's laws, lost faith in their traditions, lost faith in themselves. They ceased to be a proud, brave people, and in their bewilderment they became humble and weak. They did not understand that Nakaa was testing them by bringing them face to face with evil – and that they were failing in the test.

'But Nakaa, sitting by the gate of the Land of Shades, watched them. Each year fewer went through the gate, many more went into the Pits. When he heard Nokiki's plea for tabu on Tanakuatua he made up his mind. The people were worthless. In the beginning he banished us from the Happy Land because our ancestors broke his commands, now he will banish us from the world; so he commanded the Little Sisters to come forth from the body of Nokiki, and destroy the people.'

'Judgement Day,' said Camilla thoughtfully.

Naeta shook his head.

'Nakaa has already made judgement,' he told her. 'Now comes the day of Fulfilment.'

'I still do not understand why you are here,' Camilla told him.

'There are still some of us who honour Nakaa's laws, who may pass by the Pits and enter the Land of Shades. We accept the judgement of Nakaa; we do his will in order that when the day comes for us to be judged he will say: "You have been faithful servants," and open the door for us. That is why we have come here to help the Little Sisters.'

'How do you do that? They seem to have done very well by themselves,' she persisted.

'When you met the Little Sisters you would have sent a message telling about them, and asking for help against them. White men are clever,' Naeta acknowledged, 'perhaps they would find a way of destroying the Little Sisters here. Or you might have sent a message to bring back the ship so that you would escape the tabu – and the will of Nakaa. We have stopped that happening. We have given the Little Sisters more time to breed, and to fly away over the world. We have made sure that the tabu-breakers shall be punished.'

Camilla studied his face for some seconds.

'Do you mean that it was you who smashed the radio?' she asked.

Naeta nodded.

'That was necessary,' he said simply. He considered silently awhile, then he said: 'Now you have told me why you came to Tanakuatua, and what you planned to do here, I understand why it was the will of Nakaa that we should come here, and help the Little Sisters. It is a good work.'

'Oh,' said Camilla, noncommittally.

Naeta nodded.

'The white men,' he said, 'came upon us as a curse. They respected nothing. They destroyed our way of life, trampled on our customs. Their temptations confused our values. Their laws were the laws of their God, not ours. They did not understand things of the spirit, only of the earth. They were evil, yet they conquered, and so faith was lost. Without faith, without traditions, man is no better than an animal. He does not matter. But it is the justice of Nakaa that those who caused him to lose his faith should suffer, too. So it is a good work.'

Camilla did not look as if she followed this line of reasoning entirely, but Naeta evidently regarded it as the last word, closing the discussion. He got up, and without saying any more retreated into a small shack of branches woven with leaves close by. The other man had already taken himself off unnoticed during the talk. I threw the remaining sticks on the fire, and we lay down beside it to get what sleep we could.

I awoke to see Naeta and the other man squatting outside his hovel. They were making a meal. It appeared to consist of a coarsely ground substance of some kind mixed to a stiff mush in a cutdown tin into which each dipped his fingers in turn.

A movement beside me revealed that Camilla also was awake. We watched the two for a few moments.

'I don't think I'd fancy that muck if they offered it,' she remarked, 'but I could do with a drink of water.'

Without further hesitation, she got up to walk over and ask for some.

Naeta hesitated, then nodded, and said something to his companion. The man leant forward, unscrewed the cap of a petrol can, and poured water into two coconut shells which he handed to Camilla. Naeta watched her take them.

'Now you go away,' he said, waving his left hand in a gesture which dismissed us both.

So we went, carrying our coconut shells, back to the place where we had left our haversacks and made our breakfast on our last two bars of chocolate.

When that was finished, we looked at one another.

'Well, what do we do now?' Camilla asked.

I shrugged.

'If we could get our clothes back some way, we might have a chance,' I said. 'The insecticide won't have lost all its potency, will it?'

She shook her head.

'I noticed my belt-buckle in the ashes of the fire,' she told me.

'Oh,' I said. 'Oh.'

'There must be a way,' she said firmly.

We sat and thought about it.

'A sort of heliograph. Something that would flash in the sunlight,' I suggested.

'Do you know morse? I don't,' said Camilla.

'I know S.O.S. That ought to do,' I told her.

'*If* anyone happens to be far enough out on the beach to see here over the trees . . .'

'We might light a fire. The smoke would show them that there's someone here. Then we could try flashing the S.O.S.'

'What with?' she inquired.

'There's the foil the chocolate was wrapped in. Couldn't we make some sort of reflector with that?'

She picked up a piece, and smoothed it out, doubtfully.

'Don't heliographs have to be aligned, or something?' she asked. 'I mean you can't just waggle them about and hope they're reflecting in the right direction.'

'We ought to be able to manage that. I'll get it mounted. Then you stand so that your head's in line between it and the settlement. When it flashes in your eyes we've got the direction.'

She continued to be unenthusiastic.

'It's so chancy. First they've got to notice it. Then they've got to find the right track. Then they're liable to run into the Islanders, just as we did. And even if they don't do that, and do succeed in getting here they'll have to tackle these two – and Naeta has the revolver. Besides, you talk glibly about "mounting" the reflector – how are you going to do that? We haven't even got a penknife between us. Frankly, I don't think it begins to be on.'

'All right. Now it's your turn to suggest something,' I said.

We sat, and continued to think.

It must have been about an hour later that we heard branches crackling underfoot, and looked round to see the two Islanders approaching.

Naeta was in the lead. He wore a belt to support his machete; thrust into it handily was also the revolver. Both he and the other man were carrying short rolls of woven matting under their left arms. The difference between their present appearance and that when we had last seen them was that now their skins gleamed all over as if newly oiled. Naeta's eyes rested upon us where we sat beside the track, for a moment, but he neither checked his step nor spoke. The other man passed us as if we did not exist. As they went by we caught a whiff of the same sharp odour which had hung around our captors on the previous day.

We watched them leave the trees and climb the zig-zag path up the crater wall until they disappeared over the rim. I looked at Camilla, she shrugged. Presently she got up.

'Well, we may as well go and see what we can find,' she said.

We made our way back to the site of last night's fire, and poked around there. There was quite a collection of empty tins thrown away, and little doubt where they had come from. I had seen the same brands among our own stores. Also there was an opened case still containing half a dozen cans of corned beef intact. A bag half-full of some coarse-ground cereal, presumably that from which he had made his breakfast, lay just inside Naeta's hovel, along with a cache of tinned fruit-salad. The petrol can, we discovered, still contained some water, but there was another, smaller can that was empty. It lay on a patch of earth darkened by some liquid sinking in, looking as if it had been deliberately emptied, and then dropped.

Camilla picked it up and sniffed at it. She pulled a face, rubbed her finger on the soil, and smelled that, too. I took the can from her. It had the same sharp odour that the two men had left behind them. I nodded.

'Yes, that must be the stuff that keeps the spiders off. They didn't mean us to have any of that,' I said.

'No,' she agreed.

She looked down at the damp patch thoughtfully. The liquid had soaked well in. There was no hope of salvaging any of it.

'It rather suggests that they've no further use for it – they won't be coming back, don't you think?' she asked.

I hadn't thought of that.

'Yes, I suppose it does,' I admitted. 'They could easily have hidden the can somewhere if they wanted it.'

She lifted the can, and sniffed at it again.

'I wonder what it is. It reminds me of something . . .'

'The men we met yesterday all reeked of it,' I said.

'Yes, I know, but – no, it was like this, but not so strong. I remember half-recognizing it then . . .'

'The question is did they get it here, or did they get it some-where else, and bring it with them in the can?' I suggested. 'If they made it here, there must be some traces, which would help.'

We scoured the neighbourhood, but found nothing. After an hour we gave up, discouraged. While Camilla rekindled the fire, I bashed open a tin of bully, and we cooked it in one of the empty cans. We ate in a thoughtful silence. Camilla broke it.

'I've been thinking,' she announced. 'How would they get that juice. It's an oily stuff. It must have been pressed out in some way. But they can't have used a press . . . How else could you do it – with only primitive means?'

The only way that occurred to me was by pounding: a pestle and mortar system. I said so.

'But without a pestle or mortar,' she commented. 'Therefore you'd need some kind of natural basin – a rock basin?' She looked up at the crater wall. 'That's the only exposed rock. Sup-pose we go along the path to the foot, and then work out left and right around the wall until we meet on the other side?'

We did that – with no great hopes on my part. I was begin-ning, after twenty minutes of searching the crater side, to think that the juice must have been brought in the can after all, when a shout from Camilla which echoed back and forth between the walls sent me hurrying across to her side.

She had found it, all right. A shallow depression in the top of a rock which projected from the wall about a quarter of the way up. When I arrived she was crouched close to a pulped mass of vegetable debris which lay spilled down the slope beside it. On the ground, at the foot of the cliff lay a part of the stem of a young tree, its fibres furred out at the end.

I climbed up to look. The natural basin was excellent for the job. It even had a channel through which the juice could flow out.

Camilla held out some of the debris.

'What do you think it is! I could kick myself. It's that heather-like stuff out on the hillside. I remember smelling it now as we walked through it. And the spiders don't like it. Do you remember, their webs only came a few feet out from the trees on to it?'

We spent the rest of the day collecting great armfuls of the heather-like plants and bringing them back to be pounded. It was hard work, and not highly rewarding for the stuff was far from juicy, nevertheless, by nightfall we had extracted some three-quarters of a pint of oily liquid from it.

'That'll be enough, surely,' Camilla said as she carefully screwed the cap on to the can representing our day's labour.

That night we slept well, untroubled by the discomforts.

The next morning we woke as the sun rose, and breakfasted on one of the tins of fruit-salad. Then Camilla picked up the can of precious juice. She poured a little into her hand, sniffed at it, and pulled a wry face.

'Well, here goes,' she said, and began to smear it on.

Presently, both shining all over, and with an odour that eliminated all other smells, we collected our haversacks, and set out on the return journey.

I had, I admit, a nasty moment when the first band of spiders we met came flowing towards us, but it was unnecessary. A few inches short of our feet they stopped, seemed to mill about for a few instants, and then retreated. I heard Camilla let out a breath, and felt consoled to know that she had not been entirely confident, either.

'So far, so good,' she said. 'Now, if we don't meet any Islanders we ought to get through. I wonder how they came to know about this stuff?' she added.

'If the totem of your clan is a spider, you probably learn a lot of spider-lore,' I suggested. 'It's enough for me that it works. Let's get along while it's still potent.'

We retraced the path through the web-canopied trees. The silence there, the lack of any living creature, the slow swaying of the discarded shrouds of gossamer made the place seem even more eerie than before now that there were only two of us. Eerie, and infinitely depressing. It would have been daunting to have to travel it alone.

Camilla felt it no less. She said, in a voice that was instinctively lowered:

'And there are miles of it like this. Every moving thing wiped out. It's frightening ... As if they had been waiting – waiting patiently in their webs all these hundreds of thousands of years until something should happen which would give them power ... and then it happened: such a little thing; such a tremendous thing – the ability to co-operate ... It makes you wonder what we could do if we were *really* to co-operate.'

'Surely we've been destructive enough with partial co-operation,' I said. 'This place seems to be a terrifying argument against efficiency. Let's get on – and out of it.'

Presently we did. We reached the region where the webs were lower. Where spiders ran along overhanging fronds to drop on us – and drop off again as though they had been scalded. Confident as we were of our protection now, even their presence seemed a relief after the utter deadness beneath the web-covered trees.

Soon we were back in spider frontier territory where bands of them hunted on the ground, and sheered off as we came near.

A few hundred yards further, and we were free of them. Another quarter of a mile or so, and we were back at the spot where the Islanders had surprised us.

We agreed to turn off the beaten path there and make our way back by the route we had come. We had seen no signs of the Islanders so far on our journey, but we had little idea where the track led, nor what was at the end of it. To follow it when there was an alternative seemed like pressing our luck too far. It meant rougher going along the path we had hacked, but the further we got from their track the easier I became in mind. At length we rejoined the track along which we had started, and which would bring us out on the beach.

It did. And the first thing we saw as we emerged into the open was a small boat beyond the reef, with sails set, making towards the north-west.

'That's odd,' said Camilla. She pulled the glasses out of her haversack, and looked at it. 'It looks like our boat – only I've never seen her with the mast stepped. I can see several heads.' She turned the glasses along the shore to the point where the boat was usually drawn up. It was no longer there. She turned them further, on to our makeshift quarters.

'Not a soul in sight,' she said, in a troubled voice.

We turned and walked along the beach. As we came closer to the tarpaulin-covered piles of stores I gave a hail. There was no reply. Nobody appeared.

'They must all be working on the settlement,' I said, without much conviction. I hailed again . . .

We approached more closely. Still there was no sign of life. The place seemed entirely deserted. We went on, in silence. Twenty yards short of the encampment Camilla stopped suddenly, and pointed. Ahead of us a patch lay on the sand like a brown shadow. It began to move towards us.

'Oh, no – no!' Camilla exclaimed.

I walked on. The band of spiders came scurrying towards me, but stopped short of my feet. I went on, round the corner of the stacked cases. From there I could see into the tarpaulin-roofed space which had served as the men's dormitory.

It was difficult to make out anything in the shadow at first. But then I did . . .

I turned away. I was able to take four or five steps before I folded up, and was horribly sick.

Camilla began to approach. I waved her off.

'Don't go in there,' I was able to warn her before the next paroxysm struck me.

When I had recovered myself I went round the corner after her. I found her standing close to the blank side of the stack. Three troops of spiders were watching her keeping a foot or two away, but she took no notice of them; her attention was entirely taken up with what she held in her hands. It was a coarsely woven bag such as the Islanders had been carrying, but empty now; split from top to bottom by a single gash.

Her head turned, and her eyes met mine. I knew she was remembering, as I was, a similar sack that had lain beside the path; but that one had been full, with a content that moved slightly . . .

I looked around. Ten or twelve such discarded sacks were strewn about, each similarly gashed.

'Now we understand what he meant by "helping the Little Sisters",' she said, unsteadily. She looked at me. 'Are they all – all –?' she asked.

I nodded. The silence, and the glimpse I had had inside the encampment left no doubt of it.

'They must have come in the night, and –' She shut her eyes. 'Oh, horrible – horrible!'

For the first time since I had known her, her composure broke down.

I stood helplessly by.

The white sail on the horizon had shrunk to a dot. The Islanders were on their way home, mission fulfilled. The men who were to be like gods had met their match in Nakaa, the Judge. The Lawgiver had upheld Nokiki; the tabu on Tanakuatua had been preserved.

# Eight

It was about a week, or it may have been ten days, later – we rather lost track of the calendar – that the aircraft came.

Camilla and I were up at the settlement site working on the first nearly completed building, attempting to make it spider-proof.

We had got ourselves clothing out of the stores and re-equipped ourselves with spray guns and insecticide. The insecticide was less effective than the extract the Islanders had used, but it worked well enough, and we had several drums of it. Our first move, after using it on ourselves, had been to spray a zone about one yard wide all round the building and then wipe out all the spiders we could find inside it. That was only partially successful. For one thing, it was necessary to re-spray the barrier every day, and for another they would succeed from time to time in floating a strand of silk across it from some bush or tree, and then they had their bridge.

We could have moved northward along the coast into parts that were not yet infested, but that would have meant first cutting a path, and then humping all our supplies along it on our backs. Nor did we know how long it would be before the spiders overran that part, too. Furthermore, we had little idea of when the weather could be expected to break, but knew we should need shelter when it did. So, in the end we decided that the best course would be to finish the building, block every cranny that could admit a spider, net all the windows, fit double doors, and do all we could to assure ourselves of at least one place where we could relax in safety.

During those days we lived in a state of siege which got on my nerves. Whether it was our movements, or the sounds of our sawing and hammering that attracted the spiders I can't say, but they came, and they waited. They crowded in a stirring, shimmering line along the outer edge of the belt we kept sprayed. When one went close the stirring ceased. They stood packed as closely as pebbles on a beach, and as motionless. To the eye alone they were inert enough to be dead. It was something more than the eye which gave the feeling of the spring coiled tight, the spark withheld, immobility at high tension. Something more than sight, too, which gave a sense of thousands of eyes watching one, alert for the moment. You could throw a handful of dirt at them, and they stayed perfectly still, crowded against the invisible barrier, heads towards you, watching you unwaveringly while the dirt pattered down on them. I began to have a feeling that they were prepared to wait there until the insecticide should lose its power to deter them, and they could come pouring across the line.

In the meantime we did our best to discourage them. We took to spraying them with petrol in the evenings. They didn't like that at all, and it created havoc among them. But the next morning there were more, feeding on those that had fallen. So then we started lighting the petrol after we had sprayed. But still there were more next day . . .

As I said, the constant threat of them got on our nerves, until I wondered whether it would become obsessive – arachnophobia, perhaps. We dared not relax any of our precautions except to shed our veils and hats when we were at work, and in no danger of having them drop on us from above. All the time we had to be on watch, for almost every day they would succeed in establishing a gossamer bridge or two and start coming over, whereupon we would have to drop whatever we were doing, and tackle them with the petrol sprays. We had to sleep under meticulously arranged mosquito netting, and the first task in the morning was to scour the buiding and the ground around it for any that might have infiltrated during the night.

But our work progressed. After five or six days we had every angle of floor, walls, and roof sealed with fibre-glass, every window covered with net held taut by battens, and had devised automatic excluders for the bottom of both inner and outer doors. At last we could feel that we had a safe refuge – though we continued to use our nets at night for reassurance.

With that achieved, we turned our attention to transporting

supplies from the encampment on the shore to the settlement site. We were able to use the tractor and trailer for the actual haul, but shifting the cases, opening them, getting the contents loaded, and then off-loaded, made heavy work for two. The full trip was more than we could manage in a day.

It was at the end of our third haul that we saw it. I had just finished parking the tractor handily to the building and climbed down from the seat when Camilla on top of the loaded trailer gave a cry, and pointed wildly towards the lagoon. I clambered up beside her wondering what the fuss was about, and there it was. A small float-plane resting on the surface of the lagoon with two figures standing on one of the floats, an inflated dinghy bobbing beside them. The noise of the tractor must have drowned the sound of their engines and prevented us from hearing them.

One of the men got into the dinghy and held on to the float, steadying it for the other.

Camilla began to scramble down.

'Quick,' she said, 'we must stop them from landing.'

We raced back down the track towards the encampment. At one point it turned to give us a view. The dinghy was already more than half way to the shore. We hurried on all we could.

When we got clear of the trees the dinghy was in only two or three inches of water, and one of the men was stepping out of it. I stopped and shouted but he was too far off to hear me. I ran on. The other man got out, and they came on, wading through the shallow water, towing the dinghy behind them. Camilla and I both shouted together. This time they heard, and spotted us, and one of them waved an arm in greeting. We shouted desperately at them, and waved them off. They exchanged a word or two with one another, and then waved back cheerfully.

They left the dinghy on the wet sand and started to walk up the beach, paying no more attention to us. There was a patch right ahead of them, moving towards them. We yelled, and waved them off again. It was no good. One of them had noticed the brown patch. He said something to his companion, and leant down to examine it more closely. The patch reached his feet, and then swarmed up him without a check.

There was a scream.

The second man stared in momentary astonishment, and then

jumped forward to beat the spiders off. The first man started to collapse, the other caught, and supported him. In a moment the spiders were all over him, too. Then he screamed . . .

We stopped, and sat down on a case until we felt a bit better.

After a time Camilla, looking across the water, said:

'Can you fly a plane?'

'No,' I told her. 'Can you navigate one?'

'No,' she said.

We continued to look at the plane awhile.

'There ought to be a radio on it – oughtn't there?' she asked.

We walked along to the dinghy, keeping our eyes off the bodies. There was a radio, all right. I put on the headphones, and switched it on. A distorted voice was speaking unintelligible jargon. I waited until it seemed to have finished, pressed a switch marked 'Trans', and talked. Then I switched back to 'Receive'. The same voice was continuing its recitation in the same jargon. I had no idea whether anyone had heard me, or not.

'Do you understand how to use this thing?' I asked Camilla.

'No,' she said. But she tried – with no better result.

We gave it up for the moment, and paddled the dinghy back to the beach. Camilla made towards the encampment while I tackled the distasteful job of finding out something about the two men.

When I rejoined her:

'One of them was a licensed pilot, name of Jim Roberts,' I told her.

She nodded.

'I heard of him in Uijanji. He ran an inter-island service, mostly mails, and hospital cases, I gathered.'

'The other was called Soames. He lived in Uijanji, too. Apparently had a sideline as an accredited correspondent to a news-agency,' I added.

'If *only* they had come when we'd not had the tractor going . . . I shall begin to believe in the tabu soon,' Camilla said.

Nevertheless, that evening we were considerably improved in spirit. Someone somewhere must have been sufficiently concerned at not hearing from us to send the plane to investigate, and when that, too, failed to report it must surely lead to a serious inquiry. How soon anything would come of it seemed to depend on whether the pilot had notified his arrival at Tanakuatua by radio, or whether time would be wasted in searching for him at sea. We could only wait and see.

Five days later we had our answer in the form of three whoops from a siren which echoed back and forth across the lagoon.

We hurried down to the shore in time to see a small grey vessel drop her anchor. She had a naval look about her, as well as the white ensign at the stern. Some kind of M.T.B., I judged.

We kept on, past the encampment, down to the water's edge, and stood there waving. By now the vessel had lowered a small boat, and four men climbed aboard it. An outboard motor started up, but the boat did not come directly towards us. Instead it made for the moored plane, and circled round that once. Then it opened up and headed for the shore. We paddled out into the shallow water to meet it. It grounded gently on the sand, the four occupants staring at us incredulously, three of them with their mouths open.

We removed our hats and veils, but they looked little reassured.

'Are you Mr Tirrie?' the petty officer in charge inquired, dubiously.

I denied it.

'Tirrie is dead,' I told him. 'They're all dead, except us.'

He looked us over hesitantly, non-committally, but curiously. He would, I am sure, have been much easier in his mind if he had found us in shirts and shorts, or even in rags.

'It's the spiders,' Camilla said.

Perhaps understandably, he did not find that explanatory or reassuring.

'The spiders,' he said vaguely, disengaging his eyes from us, and letting them wander.

They came to rest on the aircraft's dinghy, and then travelled up the beach to where the bodies lay. They still looked like bodies at that distance to the casual glance, for all that the spiders would by now have left nothing but skin and bone inside the clothes.

'And those two?' he asked, looking back to us.

'The spiders got them, too. We tried to stop them ...' Camilla told him.

'The spiders,' he repeated, looking at her hard.

'Yes, there,' said Camilla pointing.

He followed the line of her finger. All he saw was an uninteresting brown patch on the sand. His expression revealed what he thought. As he turned his head he exchanged a glance with one of his companions. The man shook his head meaningly.

The petty officer made up his mind. He got to his feet.

'I'd better have a look at them,' he said.

'No,' exclaimed Camilla. 'You don't understand. They'll kill you.'

He stepped over the side of the boat.

'The spiders?' he inquired, with a deadpan look at her.

'Yes,' said Camilla. She turned to me. 'Arnold, stop him. Explain to him.'

He turned to me with a careful look. It occurred to me that he was now suspicious of us, deciding that we had a good reason for not wanting the bodies looked at closely. I tried a reasonable approach.

'Look here,' I said, 'you don't think we're dressed up like this for fun, do you? If you must go, at least take sensible precautions.'

I took off my gloves, and held them and my hat out to him.

He looked at them, half-inclined to reject them. Camilla said:

'Please, please, take them.'

With an air of humouring her, he did. He put on the hat. Camilla tied the veil round his neck, then she bent down and tucked the ends of his trousers into his socks.

'And the gloves,' she told him. 'You must keep them on.'

The other three men still in the boat were smiling a little, but with a trace of uneasiness now.

'Please get aboard,' the petty officer told us, with a glance at the men which indicated that we were to be kept aboard.

We did so, and watched him splash through the shallow water and start up the beach.

At least three bands of spiders became aware of him, and started on converging courses.

Presently the men in the boat with us became silent. They, too, had noticed them. One of the men hailed him, and pointed. The petty officer looked round, but apparently failed to notice anything unusual. He waved a gloved hand, and went on.

He reached the two bodies, and bent down, examining them.

Two of the brown patches were now quite close. The man in the boat hailed again, but the petty officer took no notice, he was looking down intently at the nearest body. Rather tentatively he stretched out a hand to touch it.

At that moment the first band of spiders reached him.

They simply flowed up, and all over him. He straightened up suddenly, and began trying to brush them off. At that moment the second and third groups arrived. They, too, came swarming up his legs.

For some seconds he stood covered in spiders except for his hat and gloves, waving his arms about in a futile attempt to get rid of them. Then he saw other groups already flowing across the sand towards him, and decided to retreat.

He came running down the beach, jumping one or two groups that were in his path, and splashed into the shallow water making for the boat. A few yards away he thought better of that and swerved aside. He went past us glistening with a carapace of living spiders.

In deeper water he flung himself down, and a lot of them were washed off. He had to submerge three times more before he got rid of the last of them.

Meanwhile, a rating had started the outboard, and we made towards him. He was standing swaying waist-deep in the water when we came up. Two of the men dragged him over the side.

'My arms,' he cried. 'Oh, God, my arms.' And he passed out.

We pulled off his jacket. Four or five spiders fell out of it, and were promptly stamped on. Evidently they had got up his sleeves, for his forearms showed a dozen red spots, and were already swelling up.

We made off at full speed for the ship.

# Nine

Well, that was the ignominious end of Lord F's Project, as such. But, of course, there was a certain amount of tidying up to be done. There were interviews for us, for instance. Our first interview, with Lieutenant-Colonel Jaye, officer commanding the combined force at Tracking Station Oahomu, could serve as prototype for the many which were to follow. It was not that he disbelieved us – after all, he had the evidence of the petty officer on his own staff, now in the sick-bay and suffering great pain in his arms – so much as that there is a difference between disbelief and incredulity; the one being rejection, the other, inability to accept. It was the latter which gave him, and others after him, so much trouble.

'Spiders,' he said, looking at us thoughtfully, 'but couldn't you just stamp on them, or something?'

We explained that they attacked in packs.

'All the same,' he said, 'surely you could have rigged up some kind of flame thrower. That ought to sizzle them up nicely.'

We agreed that it had been mooted, and that it would have had a limited use, in favourable circumstances, and we went on to explain the plan for a fire-line to check their advance, but that that would be only a temporary measure.

What, in fact, we failed entirely to convey was the scale of the infestation. It is so difficult to use the word millions without being thought to exaggerate; and advisable, we found, to eschew the word billions altogether. He obviously took our declaration that the spiders had wiped out every living creature in the parts they had overrun, to mean merely that we had not seen any other creatures.

The interview ended with him telling us:

'I am afraid you will have to stay here until I get instructions concerning you. We will try to make you as comfortable as we can.'

'Well,' said Camilla, as the door shut behind us, 'there you have us. Two people who have undoubtedly been through a very trying experience which has left them slightly off their rockers.'

His report must, however, have carried weight in some quarters, for five days later a team of four investigators flew in. One was from the Colonial Office; another a naturalist; the third, a photographer; the other, as far as I could gather, was inquiring on Lord Foxfield's behalf. They asked us a lot of questions, and treated our replies with reserve.

The following day their plane took us all to Tanakuatua, and I had my first aerial view of the island. It was the impressive way to see it. The sight of half the island tented over with its covering of web had a marked effect on our companions. Their manner towards us noticeably changed.

When we landed from a dinghy, all duly sprayed and protected, I led three of them to the encampment while Camilla and the naturalist went off along the beach, both of them slung about with specimen boxes.

At the encampment I paused, indicated the entrance and watched my three go in under the tarpaulin. I had no intention of going in there again myself. I stood outside waiting for them while one band of spiders after another ran knee-high up my legs before dropping off. Presently they came out again, all looking pretty sick.

Then I took them up to the settlement site. The spiders had got across our protective strip, and were now clustered all round, and all over, our spider-proofed building, stirring and glistening as they waited there. We stood watching them for some moments.

The Colonial Office man said, uneasily:

'It's almost as if they think there's something – or someone – in there that they want ... I suppose there's no chance ...?'

We went closer, and dispersed those round the doorway with the spray. There was, of course, no one inside the building – and no spiders, either.

'All the same, you *were* taking refuge in there ...' the same man said. He shook his head. 'I've seen enough of this place. I'm ready to go back now.'

'You may be,' said the photographer, 'but what we've got to do is convince the people back home. Not an easy job with the unsupported word – as I am sure Mr Delgrange will agree.'

He hitched the large black box he carried slung over one shoulder, round to his front and started selecting cameras and lenses from it. We watched him taking movies and stills for half an hour, until we got tired of it, then we retreated to the dinghy, the only open-air spider-free place to be found, and sat there smoking and watching bands of spiders patrol the beach while we waited.

'It looks to me,' said Lord Foxfield's man, 'as if there's only one thing to be done with this place. Spray it from the air with the strongest damned insecticide there is – every square foot of it.

The Colonial Office man shook his head.

'No good. It'd just lie on top of that canopy of web,' he decided.

'Well, wait till a gale strips that off, and then do it,' said the other.

'You'd not get them under the leaves even then. They'd sit it out,' the Colonial Office man told him. 'No, the only thing is a good dose of napalm on the windward side, when there is a good wind. Burn off the whole bloody place.'

'If it would ignite,' said the first. 'They've used napalm in jungles without burning them off.'

'Or what about just leaving them alone to work it out. After all, it stands to reason that any form of society having to depend exclusively on cannibalism must outgrow its food supply in the end.'

'We've been over all that,' I put in, and advanced Camilla's theory of the spiders learning to catch fish. 'Besides,' I added, 'the longer they exist, the more the chance of their spreading.' We were still discussing ways of dealing with them when the photographer joined us. He seemed pleased with himself.

'Now I just want one sequence showing how they attack a human being. Would one of you gentlemen oblige,' he requested.

Camilla and the naturalist came back along the beach, deep in conversation, about an hour later. The reserve with which he had treated both of us had altogether thawed. He handled the boxes they were carrying with great care.

'What have you got in there?' asked the Colonial Office man suspiciously. 'Not ...?'

'Yes. The evidence,' Camilla told him, lifting the lid. He recoiled, and then saw that the top was still covered by a wire gauze. He looked in cautiously at the milling mass of spiders. 'The Little Sisters – provisionally named *Araneus Nokikii*,' said Camilla.

We, and the four investigators, left Oahomu the following day, and flew home via Honolulu and San Francisco.

Two days after we landed we were ushered into the presence of Lord Foxfield, to give him our account of the events on Tanakuatua.

He was quite put out. From time to time he punctuated our story with exclamations: 'Tch-tch!' 'Most unfortunate!' 'Most regrettable!' and occasionally went as far as to concede: 'Terrible!'

'But surely,' he said in a puzzled way when we had ended, 'surely in spite of all the difficulties there were steps that could have been taken to avert this tragedy?'

'Possibly,' suggested Camilla, 'we were not quite enough like gods to take them.'

Our interview ended on a different note.

'I shall be instructing my solicitors to bring an action,' he told us. 'It is clear that this species of spider came into existence as a direct result of a mutation caused by the radioactive contamination of a part of Tanakuatua. The "clean" certificate which was a condition of purchase stated the existing level of radiation – and, no doubt, stated it correctly – but it also implied that the island was free from the *effects* of radiation, or such was the inference that a reasonable man might be expected to draw. In effect, then, the seller misrepresented the condition of the island to the purchaser, for the effect of the radiation was to render Tanakuatua uninhabitable, and therefore worthless to the purchaser.

'When the hearing takes place you will of course, both be called as key witnesses.'

Naturally enough, we never were called.

Owing to some political sensation at the time, the whole Tanakuatua affair had received remarkably little publicity, and the

Government had no desire to put it under the limelight. The case was settled out of court. His Lordship's purchase money was refunded, he was reimbursed for the cost of the expedition, compensation was paid to close relatives of the deceased, a gesture made towards ourselves, and, for what, all in all, amounted to a tidy charge upon the public funds, the Government found itself once more the embarrassed owner of Tanakuatua.

Just what steps were taken to rid the island of the Little Sisters I have been unable to find out, but the whole matter has been rendered academic by the Tanakuatuan eruption.

There was, it may be recalled, some preliminary confusion over that, due to the announcement of volcanic activity there being so quickly succeeded by reports from Moscow, Tokyo, and San Francisco of the low-level detonation of a fusion-bomb at approximately the same time and place. These mistakes were, of course, satisfactorily cleared up by official announcements, which added that a survey flight undertaken after the eruption had shown Tanakuatua, which was fortunately an uninhabited island, to be now devoid of any signs of life.

I still hear occasionally from Camilla, who seems to get about the world quite a lot. Mostly, her communications take the form of clippings from obscure local newspapers which, when I manage to get them translated, invariably deal with deaths attributed to spider bites.

But the latest was different. It was a small box, posted from somewhere in Peru. Inside, floating in a bottle of spirit, was a specimen which I had no doubt in identifying – and I ought to know – as a Little Sister – *Araneus Nokikii*.

Well, well . . . Time, I suppose, will show . . .

## More About Penguins and Pelicans

*Penguinews*, which appears every month, contains details of all the new books issued by Penguins as they are published. It is supplemented by our stocklist, which includes almost 5,000 titles.

A specimen copy of *Penguinews* will be sent to you free on request. Please write to Dept EP, Penguin Books Ltd, Harmondsworth, Middlesex, for your copy.

*In the U.S.A.*: For a complete list of books available from Penguins in the United States write to Dept CS, Penguin Books, 625 Madison Avenue, New York, New York 10022.

*In Canada*: For a complete list of books available from Penguins in Canada write to Penguin Books Canada Ltd, 2801 John Street, Markham, Ontario L3R 1B4.

*In Australia*: For a complete list of books available from Penguins in Australia write to the Marketing Department, Penguin Books Australia Ltd, P.O. Box 257, Ringwood, Victoria 3134.